THIS RUINED PLACE

THIS RUINED PLACE

A novel by

Michael Lawrence

8N PUBLISHING

First published by 8N Publications, 2024

This is a work of fiction. Names, characters,
places and incidents are either the products of the
author's imagination or used fictitiously.
Any resemblance to actual persons, living or dead,
events, or locales is entirely coincidental.

Cover design: Purpose on Paper
Title page drawing: Michael Lawrence

Print ISBN: 979-8-9879774-3-9
Ebook ISBN: 979-8-9879774

Here as I take my solitary rounds,
Amidst thy tangling walks and ruined grounds,
And, many a year elapsed, return to view
Where once the cottage stood, the hawthorn grew,
Remembrance wakes with all her busy train,
Swells at my breast, and turns the past to pain.

From *The Deserted Village* by Oliver Goldsmith

Contents

AUTHOR'S NOTE : ABOUT THIS BOOK

When I was a boy, my grandparents told me of a cousin who, in 1943, at the age of sixteen, vanished from the face of the earth. Until then he lived in a village in the county of Dorset in southern England. If I ever heard his name I have no recollection of it, but I do remember being told that he was very tall, with wild hair, and that he had an 'interesting nose'. And that's it. End of story, you'd think.

But many years later I came across an article about a Dorset village whose residents were evacuated by order of the government during World War Two so that it could be used for military exercises and training purposes. The village was called Tyneham and the article carried photographs that matched some of the ones that my late grandparents had shown me in their family album when talking about the obscure cousin.

Intrigued, I sought more material about the place, and soon, fascinated by what I read, I packed a bag and drove down to Tyneham, some 200 miles from where I lived at the time. There, I parked just above the village and strolled down a grassy incline between ancient trees, through a wooden gate in a low stone wall, and into...

Ruins.

Yes, Tyneham, abandoned those many years ago, was nothing now but a disorderly assortment of roofless, semi-collapsed former dwellings with weed-covered floors and ivy crawling through ragged rectangles that once were windows. And what a dismal, soulless place it was! Only two buildings still stood in their entirety: the church and the schoolhouse, which offered information about the village and the valley it huddled in, with old photographs showing how it had looked before the war, and many of the people who'd lived there.

I entered the schoolhouse: a lofty, chapel-like room with sturdy wooden beams, brass oil lamps dangling on long chains from a white-painted ceiling. A large blackboard on an easel, and an upright piano, stood either side of a brick fireplace. Rows of linked desks displayed samples of very old school work, under glass. I was looking at the work on the desks when an elderly man came in. We struck up a conversation. He too had come to look the school over, but he wasn't a casual visitor like me. He'd been a pupil there. He told me how it had been for him and the people who lived in Tyneham, giving me a first-hand view of life there, in his day, for the ordinary family. It had been far from easy for most working people, he said. There'd been little money, few luxuries, no electricity, running water, flush toilets, radio, and most of the other things that we take for granted nowadays. He was cynical, too, about the class divisions built into such communities; an alternative view to the slightly romantic picture that I'd naively formed from much of what I'd read of life there, which painted Tyneham as an idyllic, nigh-on-perfect place – not the case at all, according to my new acquaintance.

In the years since that first visit of mine – I've been back several times – little has changed in Tyneham. There have been attempts to tidy it, with many of the old buildings shored up and made safe (though not rebuilt) so that visitors may walk in and out of them and take photographs without risk. But the village and the Tyneham Valley have been in military hands for eight decades now, and there are still jeeps there, and barbed wire, and signs warning visitors to watch where they go if they value their lives and limbs.

Over time the idea grew in me that I might write a novel set in a place modeled on Tyneham in which an elderly man who'd lived there as a boy goes back there for a very specific reason in the August of 1999. When I finally resolved to attempt this I decided to pay the place a further visit in the cause of making my descriptions as accurate as possible. Along the way I stopped off at Lyme Regis, a pleasant seaside town famous for a certain iconic scene in the film of John Fowles' novel 'The French Lieutenant's Woman'. There I walked down to the great sweeping harbor and along the old stone jetty known as The Cobb, and parked myself near the end of it on a bench, to eat a sandwich while watching the leaping waves. Sitting there I noticed, on the back of the bench, a plaque dedicated to a local man by the name of

Juby Wiscombe. I'd never heard the name Juby before, but it appealed to me and I decided to give it to the old man in my story. His other name, his surname, came from what I was sitting on. So it was that Juby Bench came to life within yards of where a storm-swept Meryl Streep stood in a hooded cape gazing out to sea in 1981. Another name came to me before I left that seat; that of the main female character I had in mind for the story. I called her Evy Cobb.

In some respects Juby Bench reflects the man I met in the schoolhouse on that first visit to Tyneham. Both in their seventies, they both returned to the village regularly, but their views on what life was once like there were, and are, very different. While the man in the schoolroom had his nostalgia well under control, Juby does not. In my book it's another character, an old friend of Juby's, who shares Schoolroom Man's views.

In the novel, the village is called 'Rouklye' (pronounced *rook*-lee). I've changed one or two other names too, but have retained those of many of the people who lived in and around Tyneham until a few turbulent days before Christmas 1943. Given the book's setting, 'This Ruined Place' seems the perfect title.

I wonder what the nameless cousin would have made of all this?

1

It's August, another dazzling August, and if I half close my eyes it's as if no time has passed, no time at all. It has, of course. Can't deny it for long. I'm Evy Cobb these years, a different person in so many ways, with a different name, different values, different hair even – and two fast-growing sons. I've told my boys about this place, told them often, but they're young, they never pay much attention. Someone else's life, a little bit of Mom's past, let her get on with it. They seem a bit more interested now that they're here, though, which pleases me. I encourage them and their dad to wander off, explore, experience as much as the authorities allow. I'll meet them back at the car in an hour, I tell them, but not to rush for the sake of it. An hour should be enough for me to do my own wandering. My more specific wandering. For my mind to fill up once again with all that happened here the last August of the old century, twenty-one years ago. Twenty-one almost to the day.

She was Midge then. Midge Miller, sixteen, and she hadn't

laughed for a week. But even she couldn't help a tiny chirrup at the sight from her window. Across the road, a prehistoric car had just pulled up outside the inn or hotel or whatever it was, and the old boy struggling to get out of it, straightening up, revealed himself to be one of the tallest men she'd ever seen, which made his car seem one of the smallest.

'Juby!'

She jumped – hadn't heard the floorboards – but before she could turn, Inger was crouching at her shoulder, also peering out.

'I was beginning to wonder if he was going to give this year a miss. He's usually here before the second week. Must be slowing up at last. Or do I mean down, I can never remember.'

'You know him?' Midge asked.

'Oh, yes. Indeed. He and Edwin were boys together. Juby comes over from Sweden every August to prowl around their childhood haunts.'

'Sweden? He lives in Sweden? Isn't that your neck of the woods?'

Inger laughed. 'Not quite the neck. The general geographic proximity, you might say.'

'If he's such an old friend why doesn't he stay here? You have another guest room.'

'Stay here? Oh no. Him and Edwin. Tuh! The tension when they're together, you could cut it with scissors.'

They watched the incredibly tall man lean into the car

for the jacket that matched his sagging black trousers. As he attempted to put the jacket on, all arms and elbows that seemed uncertain which way to go, Inger rose from her crouch.

'What I came up for,' she said, 'was to ask if you're helping in the shop again today.'

Midge stiffened. Thumb and fingertips of one hand on the window glass. Five tense digits. The other five a claw at her side. It was like being at home. You always had to be *doing* something. Couldn't just sit at a window minding your own business, oh no. Criminal offence, looking out of a fucking window.

'If you like.'

'It's not compulsory,' Inger said with a very slight edge.

Midge let her hand fall from the glass; tried to sound less fed up.

'No. Really. I don't mind.'

'When you're ready then. No rush.'

Then she was alone again, watching the ungainly old man negotiate the doorway of The Ferryman. To pass through the entrance – low even for people of normal height – he had to drop his head to shoulder level, but as his shoulders were higher than the top of most men's heads he still managed to crack his skull. Again she laughed. Whoa, two laughs in two minutes. A laugh a minute, have to watch that, people might think that being abandoned by your parents is fun.

Her parents. Her fists involuntarily clenched at the thought of them. Mostly they shuffled papers at the *Earthsave International* offices near home in Winchester, but every so often some Big Threat to humanity would crop up somewhere in the world and they'd be off with a boatload of other heroes to try to prevent it, frustrate it, aggravate its perpetrators. This time it was some lunatic dictatorship (the Inanians, her dad called them) testing their latest weapon of mass destruction in the South Pacific. The long-promised trip to Orlando had been scrapped and they'd cast about for somewhere to deposit her. Usually when they went on these missions she was left with Nessa and her folks, but the Friedmans had gone away a couple of days before the Inanian thing came up, which reduced the alternatives to one.

Here. A room above a bookshop in South Dorset. Her grandparents'.

She hadn't been here often over the eight years she'd been forced to live in this country. Didn't know them very well really. But eight years! Damn near a hundred months, almost four hundred weeks, never mind the hours, the minutes. An eternity. She didn't fit here. She wasn't *of* this piddling little country. She longed, just *longed*, to be back in Michigan, where the girls she'd grown up with still lived, still laughed, had good times, and the rest.

It was her mother's fault. Her fault for being English, getting homesick, bringing them to the dismal little land of her birth so that so she could be happy again. Never mind the *daughter's* happiness. The years in which she, Midge, had to not only live here but learn to sound like she *belonged* here so that ears wouldn't prick up whenever she spoke and people ask what the hell kind of accent that was and where the hell she came from.

She turned from the window, into the gloomy little cell she'd been sentenced to for she didn't know how long. They'd made it plain, her parents, that they thought more of the welfare of others than of hers. Didn't they realize how screwed up that was? How it screwed *her* up, knowing that their efforts to protect the planet were the real reason her school work was suffering? She'd tried telling them, but she always came badly out of such confrontations. Compared with their 'humanitarian objectives', her pitiful attempts to present her case made her sound like a self-centered brat.

'If no-one reacted against such things, Midge,' her mother had said, 'the world would be right up shit creek.'

'It *is* up shit creek, you're always saying.'

'Yeah, but someone has to try to make things better.'

'Well, why can't it be someone *else*?'

'If we all said that, darling, nothing would ever improve.'

The end result of which was that she 'must be strong'; look beyond her 'own domestic preferences': arguments she had no option but to submit to.

She dashed an arm across her eyes and allowed them a watery inspection of the room. What a hovel. No carpet, just a big square rug on bare brown boards: a thin faded thing with unraveling ends that she longed to tug till there was nothing left. Ornaments included an ancient jug-and-bowl set (bowl cracked, jug the last resting place of a dead spider), a pair of dusty china dogs, fragments of rock on every flat surface, a wooden chess set with a piece missing. On the walls, in thin black frames, there were a couple dozen old photos that held no interest whatsoever. The pictures were wonky, all of them, and wonky they would stay. Nothing to do with her.

Then there was the mirror: a full-length mahogany chevalier which seemed to catch her reflection wherever she went about the room, like it was watching her. It was her general practice to avoid mirrors as much as she could. The sly peek before going out was rarely more than that; just a glance to make sure there was no sleep in her eyes, food lodged between her teeth, that her hair was reasonably tidy, and so on. Mirrors were a curse. They revealed what everyone saw when they looked at her: gawky frame, too-wide shoulders, big nose, patchy complexion prone to spottiness, hair like tangled rope if she didn't wash it daily. If she didn't look quite as bad in the chevalier it wasn't because its old specked glass possessed some special quality or power, it was merely that it reflected a different arrangement of light and shade than more familiar rooms. Maybe the girl in the mirror is the real Midge, she thought. The Midge in the mirror smiled. Clearly she'd been thinking that too.

Then they both turned, one to the left, one to the right, and went out to their separate landings, where at least one smile quickly faded. Midge couldn't speak for the real her in the mirror, but her day did not look promising. She might have viewed it with more optimism – or at least more interest – if she'd known that it would be a day that would reshape her life. Set the wheels in motion anyway.

And all without mirrors.

2

Her grandparents, Inger Bjølstad and Edwin Rainey, had been together, unmarried, for over forty years. Inger saw no point in marriage and insisted on her surname being used on all documents and communications. 'We're two separate people,' she said, 'two *single* people, and we'll be treated as such.' Almost every adult who knew them on anything approaching a personal basis called them by their first names. So did Midge, but only in her head. She'd known them all her life, yet felt that she knew them hardly at all. Visits to them or by them had never been frequent, so until now, this week, she'd spent little time alone in their company. Without her parents there they made her nervous, especially Inger, who could be quite spiky when crossed. Midge had witnessed her anger with Edwin a couple of times and hoped she herself would never be on the receiving end of it. She loved the way her grandmother spoke, however. Her accent was slight, her English more precise than most English people's, but every now and then she would put a Scandinavian spin on a word that suddenly made her seem like the most colorful person around. Which she probably was anyway in a hole like Underthorpe.

Inger was removing the old display from the shop window to make way for a new one while Midge went from shelf to shelf putting newly-delivered titles in alphabetical order. She was helping out because she felt obliged to. A way of earning the keep she didn't want. She could think of any number of things she'd rather be doing. No. Correction. She couldn't think of one, here.

'Midge, we have a visitor!'

The shop door sprang back and the hyperactive brass bell drowned out the thud of forehead smacking lintel. The incredibly tall man's knees folded and he staggered in clutching his head, one leg trying to walk away from him. If he'd been a character in a comic he would have had a halo of stars whizzing round his head. Inger jumped back from the window and threw a chair under the graceless giant just in time to stop him crashing to the floor.

'Juby Bench, how many years have I had this shop?'

He groaned. 'Please, not a quiz, spare me, woman.'

'And how many times have you banged your head on that door?'

'Can't remember, it's all that banging me head on the bleedin' door.'

He removed his hand from his forehead and looked at it. There was nothing in it, but on his brow there was a reversed OU where it had rushed at the embossed MIND YOUR HEAD above the door.

'Bloody country. Everything's so *low* here.'

'Sit quiet a moment,' Inger commanded.

'I thought I was.' He scowled about him. The shop interior must have seemed very dull after the brilliant light outside. He peered Midge's way through the comparative gloom. 'Who's that?'

'Midge,' Inger said. 'She's staying with us for a while.'

'Midge?'

'Midge Miller, my granddaughter from Winchester. Midge, come and meet Mr. Bench.'

'Juby,' the old man said. 'Just Juby.'

As she approached he raised his rump two inches off the chair and extended a startlingly long arm. The wrist on the end of the startlingly long arm was like a dog's favorite bone, while the palm that swamped hers was as smooth as a piece of worn old leather that's been left out in the sun. The knobbly fingers closed lightly but firmly, jerked her hand up and down twice, and withdrew. Then Juby Bench sat back and studied her.

'Does she look like your girl?' he asked.

'She has her height,' Inger said. 'And Kristin's eyes, I

think. Not her nose, though. That's all her own.'

'Don't talk to me about noses,' Juby Bench said.

Inger laughed. So did he. Obviously an old joke between them. His nose wasn't one you could ignore. Midge had always been self-conscious about her own nose, but hers was positively petite beside his great beak. His eyes had not left her. Very pale gray eyes. Unnerving, the way they examined her.

'Midge, was it?' he said.

'Yes.'

'Like the insect?'

'Lost none of your charm over the past year, I see,' Inger said to him.

He ignored this. 'Why would anyone call their daughter Midge?'

'It's a nickname.' Inger again.

'Nickname?'

'She was a very small toddler.'

'She's not a toddler now, or small. What's your given name?' he asked Midge.

'Evy,' said Inger.

He flashed her an annoyed glance. 'Doesn't the girl have a tongue?'

'You're making her uncomfortable, can't you see?'

'Me? Making her uncomfortable?' To Midge: 'I'm not, am I?'

He was, but she wasn't going to admit it. 'No.'

'Midge,' he murmured, turning the name over in his mouth like a boiled sweet he wasn't sure about. He shook his head. 'Nah. Doesn't fit. Not the young lady I see before me. I'll call you Evy. Much better.'

'She might not want you to call her Evy,' Inger said.

The exceedingly pale eyes drilled a silent question into Midge's own. She shrugged off-handedly. She didn't care what he called her; just wished he'd stop looking at her that way.

'How's the head?' Inger asked their visitor, tactfully obliging him to release her granddaughter from his gimlet gaze.

'Oh, wonderful,' he replied. 'If it belonged to someone else.'

Midge escaped to her shelves while she had the chance. From there, watching the pair of them between and around books, she saw Inger reach out and touch the old man's cheek, a cheek of white bristles, very delicately, like someone attempting Braille for the first time.

'Why so late this year, old fella?' Almost a whisper.

'Less of the old,' he said.

'You're usually here before now.'

'I've been a bit...'

'A bit what?'

'Under the weather.'

'Oh, nothing serious, I hope.'

'If it was, you think I'd tell you? You'd send me straight

to bed with a thermometer and a bunch of grapes.'

'But you're staying to the end of the month?'

'Can't say.'

'You're not usually so vague either.'

Juby Bench gripped his knees to ease himself upward. His joints creaked as he rose. On his feet, he was forced to stoop in the low room, the ceiling flattening his unruly shock of wiry gray hair. He settled his jaw on one shoulder and his lips moved as though preparing to pass words, but then clamped shut. His eyes cut across to Midge, who tried to look engrossed in her work. He wants to tell Gran something, she thought, something personal, but he can't with me here.

It wasn't that. It was nothing like that. But it would be several days before she discovered what was on Juby Bench's mind, and then she would be sworn to secrecy, unable to share it with anyone. Anyone at all.

3

It was perhaps a slight overstatement to say that Midge hadn't laughed for a week. There'd been the odd reluctant snicker; always her grandfather's doing. Edwin Rainey had a way of making a joke of things that even Midge, determined to appear displeased when eyes were upon her, found hard to resist. He was especially entertaining when taking off

Inger in one of her outbursts at the posturings of some 'idiot politician' on the radio or some foolish enquiry in the shop. When Inger was at her most agitated Edwin would stand behind her mimicking her outrageously, flapping his arms, juggling his eyebrows, and when she whirled round suspecting something of the sort there he'd be examining his fingernails and humming quietly. He also seemed to find it impossible to walk across a room like a normal person. He had an entire range of silly walks. Sometimes he did a duck waddle, sometimes a high-kicking ostrich, sometimes he plodded around like an elephant. He did voices too. In fact he rarely used his own when she was about. She had two favorites: the dive-bomber whine and the John-Wayne-with-a-hangover growl. Inger wasn't amused by any of this. She must have heard it all, seen it all, countless times over the years. But her irritation didn't bother Edwin. On the contrary, he seemed to revel in it.

Most days he was already in the kitchen when Midge went down for breakfast, but the first she saw of him that morning was around eleven, shortly after Juby Bench went back to The Ferryman. Still in the shop, she was arranging special offers on a small bookcase beside the desk, when she heard the back door open, followed by the thump of something weighty being dropped. Then Edwin was ambling along the short passage between the shop and the kitchen and looking in.

'I'm back.'

Inger, putting the finishing touches to her window display, said: 'You've been somewhere?'

'Fishing. Since dawn. You must have noticed I wasn't here.'

She looked at Midge. 'I don't think we did, did we?'

Midge cleared her throat discreetly.

'Well, I've got our tea out here,' Edwin said. 'Nice pair of ripe young perch. Fish pie tonight.'

'We'll look forward to it,' Inger said. 'Should be home by tea-time.'

He frowned. 'You're going somewhere?'

'We are. Very soon.' Inger stepped back, appraising her handiwork. In a minute she would assess it from the street, the only view that really counted. 'Which means,' she said, 'that you must mind the shop.'

Edwin's look of horror was a picture. 'Me? No chance. Put up the closed sign, it's your business, I'm retired.'

Inger plunged her hands into the deep pockets of her salmon pink dungarees and turned to him with a studiedly patient air.

'Edwin.'

'Don't Edwin me,' he said. 'What did I sell the last time you left me in charge? One lousy picture postcard, and it wasn't even a local.'

'That was April, this is August. In August, with the stock that's just come in, and my discounts, even you can't fail.'

Edwin sighed – and gave in. There could only be one

winner in arguments between these two, it seemed to Midge. Same one every time.

'Where you off to then?'

'You don't want to know,' Inger said.

Which made him even more curious. 'Come on, where?'

'Picnic.'

'Picnic?'

'With Juby.'

Edwin took a long breath. 'When did he turn up?' His voice had gone quite cold.

'Checked in across the road a couple of hours ago.'

'Damn him, I was going over there for a bite.'

'You'll be able to when we've gone. I'll allow you to shut the shop for half an hour. No more, mind.'

'Is he never going to stop these bloody pilgrimages?' Edwin said. 'I imagine that's where you're going?'

'Where else? You know Juby.'

His shoulders slumped and, glancing at Midge from beneath exaggeratedly defeated brows, he shuffled out as Poor Little Browbeaten Man. For once there was nothing amusing in his performance.

When she next saw him she was at the kitchen table wrapping the sandwiches Inger had started and left her to finish when she went through to the shop to see who'd just entered it. 'How ya doin', kid?' enquired the hoodlum from an old film noir who'd just rattled down the back stairs to the kitchen.

'Okay,' she felt obliged to say.

Edwin reached for the bread knife, sawed off the end of the remaining third of the loaf, lathered it with butter, and was about to sink his teeth into it when a large shape filled the entrance to the passage from the shop.

'Ed,' Juby Bench said in somber greeting.

Edwin set his snack aside untasted, wiped buttery fingers on the seams of his trousers.

'Here again then, Jube.'

Juby clumped down the two stone steps into the kitchen. The lower floor allowed him to raise his head, but even here the ceiling flattened his gray mane. Brittle flakes of dry old paint spattered the shoulders of his black jacket like dandruff.

'Here again, boy. Keeping well?'

'Mustn't grumble,' Edwin said. 'Yourself?'

'Could grumble, no point.'

After which they seemed to have nothing to say to one another. Silence fell like a ton of cottonwool bricks as the two men, absolute physical opposites – the one unnaturally lanky with a mass of out-of-control hair, the other short, pot-bellied and bald – virtually froze, avoiding eye-contact. Midge was grateful when Inger breezed in blowing dust off the cane picnic hamper she'd just emptied of old receipts and invoices.

'All done?' she asked Midge.

While they packed the hamper, Edwin and Juby

remained where they were, as if turned to wax. Inger, obviously used to such behavior when these two were together, did not remark on this. Only when everything was ready, the hamper closed, did she demand action.

'Come along now,' she said briskly to Midge and Juby, 'or we'll be lunching at four. Edwin: sell books. That is your sole purpose in life today.'

'How am I supposed to mind the shop *and* cook for tonight?' Edwin said.

'Just worry about the shop. I never liked fish pie anyway.'

'You didn't? You don't? You've never said. All these years, and you've never told me that?'

'I didn't want to hurt your feelings.'

Inger touched her lips with her fingertips, then his forehead, as though dispensing a blessing. He didn't react, but as Midge followed the others out, she glanced at him to nod farewell. He was staring at the door Inger and Juby had left by, on his face an expression of cold fury.

4

Having been parked in the sweltering sun all morning, Inger's eight-year-old-blue Volvo was like an oven inside. Juby Bench asked Midge if she would like to sit in the front, but Inger wouldn't hear of it – 'She'll be fine in the back, won't you, Midge?' – so he took the passenger seat while Midge clipped herself into the one behind him. Before moving off, Inger plucked her sunglasses from the folding visor over the windscreen. The silver frames, plunging into the thick dark hair over her ears, emphasized the hank of white that sprang from her crown. Midge sifted through her shoulder bag for her own glasses. They weren't there, and now they were off and it was too late to go back for them. Knowing she hadn't got her shades, the light became all the brighter. Painfully so.

Last night Inger had taken the precaution of draping a towel over the steering wheel, but it was still too hot to grip, so her fingers danced on the wheel for the first half-mile or so, as she chattered constantly, loudly, exhilaratedly. Juby's conversation was more measured, but Midge, feeling about four years old strapped in the back, scowled at the back of his head, his long neck, creased as an old map, shirt collar in need of a wash. He was an intruder. She didn't want him there. Didn't want any of them.

Once out of Underthorpe the road dipped and wound through hills and hollows divided by drystone walls and fields of various shades and hues. Virtually blinded by the dazzling white escarpment of a chalk quarry, Midge hunched low in her seat for most of the journey, arms folded, sighing with unmitigated boredom at all the scattered farmsteads, the steeples of churches, the brown thatch of cottages, isolated clumps of woodland on horizons, until, between hills, she glimpsed the sea. This brought her to immediate attention, straining for a better view. She'd forgotten how close Underthorpe was to the coast. She loved the sea, but hardly ever got this near to it, and in all the years of brief 'duty visits' down this way, no one had ever taken her there. Well, perhaps today they would. This place they were going to (the village Juby and Edwin lived in as boys), maybe it was on the coast. If so, the day might not be quite such a washout after all.

When, without warning, Inger span the wheel and the Volvo jerked onto a descending side road, Midge was the only one who was not prepared. She gave a little shriek and rocked rapidly about while reaching in several directions at once for something to hold on to. By the time she'd grabbed the shoulders of the seat in front they were through a short tunnel of trees and flying between unplowed fields defined by barbed-wire fences and gates that bore enamel signs showing a silhouetted walking man, and the words:

MILITARY FIRING RANGE
KEEP OUT

The first of these signs brought a sharp two-word retort from Juby Bench, which sent Midge's eyes flying to the mirror, to meet Inger's – who immediately diverted her own gaze to the windscreen. Barren fields, barbed-wire, warning signs, none of it mattered, though, for directly ahead sat a cone of brilliant blue, shimmering between ochre cliffs. She leant forward as the road rose and fell, twisted and turned, yet always delivered them back to this excellent course. They never seemed to get much closer, but it couldn't be far now, minutes, surely, and she'd be strutting along the beach with sand between her toes, or kicking pebbles, inspecting shells like a five year old.

'Here we are!' Inger cried suddenly.

Midge craned her neck. They were approaching a low stone wall behind which stood the disheveled walls of a linked row of ruined cottages. The sea had disappeared, and for a moment it looked as if the road, along with the car, would end at the wall, but both veered sharply to the left and carried them past a small pond and a group of trees, up an incline to an open plain of stony ground. Inger found a place well away from a number of other parked cars, jerked hers to a halt, and switched the engine off with a flourish. At once, with the urgency of someone keen to vomit, Juby Bench threw his door open and leapt out. Inger got out at a more dignified pace, while Midge remained in her seat, fed up. So much for the sea.

'Coming, Midge, or staying here all day?'

She unclipped her belt and got out, hoping her displeasure showed. The sun smacked the top of her head like a reprimand. After the breeze through the open windows the heat was unbelievable. She screwed her eyes up against the light. They were in a wide valley of sorts, encircled by green hills. Nothing much else to see, anywhere. Juby seemed to have found something to look at, though. He stood stock-still, as he had earlier when stuck for words with Edwin, gazing down the slope toward the ruins they'd passed on the way to the car park. Midge heard Inger hauling the hamper out of the boot, made a duty-move to help, but her grandmother, no malingerer, tossed a tartan blanket onto the car roof, jammed a straw hat with a crimson bandana on her head, and slammed the boot.

'Spot of shade, I think. Down there?'

She indicated the grove of trees between the car park and the ruined buildings. Midge shrugged. Wherever. All the same to her.

'Juby?'

At the sound of his name, Juby set off down the slope like one who's been kicked sharply. In spite of the heat he still wore his enormous black jacket, which, unbuttoned, flapped about him like badly-coordinated wings.

'You could always carry this as you're going that way!' Inger bawled after him. He kept going without any kind of acknowledgement. 'Just us then,' she said to Midge, 'bring the blanket, will you,' and started toward the trees, the hamper bumping against her leg.

'What about the windows?' Midge said, tugging the blanket off the roof.

'Windows?'

'They're still open.'

'Leave 'em. Be hot as Hades in there when we get back, even with them open.'

Midge set off after her, the hot blanket rough against her bare arms. When they reached the trees and shade, they opened the blanket and spread it across the flattest section of grass they could find. There was no sign of Juby Bench.

'Where did he go?' she asked.

Inger dropped to her knees and threw back the lid of the hamper. 'He'll be wanting to see what they've been up to since last year.'

'What who's been up to?'

'Who? Why, the – tuh!' She broke off. A bee had landed on the sandwiches and seemed keen to get inside the silver foil. 'Oh no you don't, you little...'

She found a stick and tried to coax the bee away without hurting it. When it transferred its attention to the stick, she tossed it away, the bee still clinging to it. Seconds later, a Scottish terrier bounded from behind a nearby tree, seized the stick in its jaws, and ran round in several joyous circles before dropping it with a yelp and scampering back the way it had come, cured of sticks for life.

Asked if she would prefer a tuna or a cheese sandwich, Midge took the cheese and a bag of crisps.

'You like picnics?' Inger asked as they settled down to eat.

'Can't remember the last one,' she answered around a

mouthful.

The last one. She must have been half her present height. Mom and Dad weren't big on days out. But here she was, suddenly picnicking after all these years, and sea or no sea it felt rather pleasant in the shade of these laden boughs. Her grandmother sat a few feet away, supporting herself with the heel of her left hand as she nibbled round the crusts of the sandwich in the other. It was quite a thing to see this generally restless woman so relaxed, but as she didn't know her well enough to feel comfortable with her silence, Midge grabbed the first subject that came to mind.

'Those signs we passed on the way. All the barbed-wire and stuff...'

'MoD,' said Inger, still nibbling.

'Sorry?'

'Ministry of Defense. This is a military zone. Army training and weapons testing ground.'

Midge peered out from their shady enclosure. What was she on about? Private cars came and went as they pleased, families strolled with cameras, kids ran all over the place, squealing. She could see the roof of a small church amid the trees beyond the ruined cottages, and many more trees all around, with bits of other buildings showing here and there, while to her right, on the hillside, cows grazed undisturbed. Military zone? Army training ground? Weapons?

Her puzzlement had been observed. 'This is the Rouklye Valley,' Inger said, as if that explained everything. It did not.

She saw this as well. 'Oh, I was forgetting. Another time, as far as you're concerned. Before my time too, really. Well, never mind, ancient history, let's just enjoy our day.'

She leant forward to pour tea from the flask into one of the three plastic cups they'd brought, handed it to Midge, then poured one for herself and set it in a hollow she created for it in the blanket. She'd barely done this when a large multi-colored ball careered down the slope from the car park, glanced off a tree, and sent the cup flying. Midge expected her to leap to her feet, as her mother would certainly have done, and dab furiously at the wet patch on the blanket while glaring at the small boy who ran to retrieve the ball. But Inger Bjølstad and her daughter were two very different kettles of fish. All Inger did was change the angle of her hat, sigh as the boy scuttled back to his parents with his ball, and pat the spilt tea with a couple of the paper napkins.

They'd just about settled down again when Juby Bench emerged from a wooded area some way below them, to their left. While not welcoming his return, the look of him took Midge by surprise. The upright determined figure that had stalked away now appeared very downcast, arms hanging limply at his sides as he stumbled up the uneven slope. He said nothing as he seated himself on a corner of the blanket and crossed his legs at the ankle. His feet, bare in open-toed sandals which, like him, had seen better days, were enormous, with long jagged toenails.

'Is it much changed since last year?' Inger asked him.

Juby stared blankly at her as if defeated by the question, then turned away, began tearing at the grass around his feet. Midge, glancing his way half a minute later, saw him stop what he was doing, frown at his hands as though catching them in some antisocial act, and gently gather up the torn blades of grass and place them, very precisely, side by side as if hoping they would grow again if treated with care.

He perked up a bit when he finally got to work on the sandwiches, which he gobbled, and the tea, which he slurped. He seemed much more at ease by the time he started on the apple Inger cut into pieces for him with a small pearl-handled knife she carried in a suede sheath for such purposes. He still didn't have much to say, but Midge began to get used to his being there. She could put up with him as long as she didn't have to talk to him. Then Inger spoiled everything.

'Midge hasn't been here before, Jube. Why don't you give her the guided tour?'

Her heart plummeted as the tousled head and the great beak of a nose turned, and those sharp pale eyes settled on her.

'She might not want a guided tour,' he growled.

'Midge?' Inger said.

The prospect of being shown round a crummy old village by this peculiar man didn't thrill her at all, but she wasn't good at saying no, so...

'Don't mind.'

He was on his feet in a trice, so eager to get going that Midge was forced to cram the last of her crisps in her mouth and also rise.

'You?' Juby asked Inger.

'I've seen it.'

She fell onto her elbows, then to her back, and tugged her hat over her eyes, dismissing the pair of them. Juby took his jacket off and dropped it on the grass, then loped away rolling up the sleeves of his off-white shirt.

'Gra-an,' Midge hissed.

Inger raised the brim of the hat. 'Yes, my darling?'

The look in her shaded eyes suggested that she knew very well how uncomfortable Midge was about this, and found it amusing.

'Oh, *forget* it.'

Never before had she spoken that way to her grandmother, but she was too angry to care if she caused offence. She swung about and headed after Juby Bench wondering what the hell you talk about to an old weirdo like him.

5

Juby stopped at the little pond they'd passed on the way to the car park. On the far side of it a man in a blue T-shirt emblazoned with the words SUNSHINE STATE leaned over to take photographs of bulrushes. There were no bulrushes on Juby's side of the pond, but there were reeds and water lilies, which he stood gazing down at. He was speaking even before Midge caught up with him.

'... a bit since I was a lad. Nothing to take snaps of then. It was a watering hole where the cattle stopped off for a drink on the way to milking. Horses too.'

'Oh, you milked horses back then, did you?' she muttered to herself.

'Wasn't clean like this, nothing like as clean. Between winter and spring, masses of frogs, casting their spawn on the surface – like transparent jelly, it was, really slimy – and we'd dip our hands in and pull it around, have races with it along the banks, dragging it.' He fell silent for a moment, then added: 'And eels.'

'Eels?' Midge said dutifully.

'Thick with 'em, here. Only little ones, but slippery old boys, not easy to catch, you had to trick them.' He glanced at her. 'What we did was, we bound up hazel twigs and sank them in the water for a day or so, then we'd hoik 'em out, quick as winking, and those bundles'd be full to bursting. Good bait, eel. The mackerel could never resist a bit of nice fresh eel. Some always found their way into the pot, though. Very tasty, eels, done right.'

With this he stalked away, toward the low stone wall that skirted the linked row of ruined buildings. This time

Midge dallied, but it was an unnoticed rebellion, and a short-lived one because she didn't know the man, had no idea how his temper worked. Some way ahead, he reached the wall and paused to peer over it at an antiquated telephone kiosk, a cream-and-red affair topped with a spike like the business end of a spear. Within the wall's perimeter, visitors ambled in and out of the ruins, touching the old stones and taking pictures as if at the Parthenon or the Coliseum or something. One couple in particular caught Midge's eye as she drew near, a man and woman, probably in their late twenties, she very much overweight and looking it in a scarlet-and-green blouse and tight white leggings that bulged in all the wrong places, he shorter and considerably thinner, in khaki shorts and a pink shirt that clashed horribly with his ginger hair. He must have announced that he wanted to take his beloved's picture, because she positioned herself in the doorless doorway of one of the cottages, one knee raised, the sole of her shoe against the stone, a podgy hand behind her head like an old-time pin-up. 'Say Mozzarella,' the photographer said, and his model giggled, and he took the picture.

As Midge joined Juby, he indicated the telephone kiosk on the other side of the wall, and said: 'I did that.'

There was a 'Closed' sign on the glass-paneled door. Through the glass Midge saw an old black phone with A and B buttons.

'Did what?'

Reaching over the wall, Juby traced a crack in one of the panels.

'When I was fifteen. Threw half a brick at it.'

'Why did you do that?'

'Why?' A surprised glance; stupid question. 'I was fifteen.'

He was about to lead the way through a gap in the wall where a small gate must once have been when the bonny young woman who fancied herself as a glamour girl launched herself toward it, followed by her partner. Juby stood aside to let them through. They gave no sign of noticing either him or his small courtesy, or even his 'The pleasure's all mine,' to their ill-matched backs.

There were several adjoining cottages beyond the wall. A much smaller building at the near end of them, a shed of sorts, was the only one with a door and roof. The roof was topped with crudely-cut gray slate, and on the equally rustic door, which was padlocked, a notice asked visitors not to pick the wild flowers, a request that might have amused Midge if she'd been in an easily-amused mood because there were no flowers in the immediate vicinity, wild or tame.

Juby had gone straight to the second cottage along, where he stooped to look in the doorway. 'Post office and village shop,' he informed her as she drew near.

He ducked inside. Following with a long-suffering sigh, she found a crumbling interior open to the skies, ivy reaching across exposed walls to which ragged portions of ancient plaster clung, an iron fire-grate teetering on a ledge where a ceiling and upper floor had once been, and beneath their feet ailing weeds between uneven gray paving slabs, while year-old leaves crunched underfoot. The place smelt of nettles and moss, the dust of an overheated summer.

'Looks bigger empty,' Juby said. 'When the counter was in, shelves stocked, customer or two chatting, it was a right jam in here.'

Sunlight entered the broken building in tall bright spirals, picking out hovering dust motes. Watching the dust's leisurely dance, Midge's mind wandered. Her thoughts were still adrift when the whispers started. Whispers so indistinct that they registered only gradually; but once her attention was caught she glanced about for whoever it was that had followed them in.

There was no one, no one else, just the two of them. The whispers faded.

' – get anything here,' Juby was saying. 'The women bought their wool here, their needles and thread, cleaning materials, candles, matches. Men bought their baccy and bootlaces. There were sweets behind the counter in big glass jars, sides of bacon on hooks, cheese and butter in slabs to be sliced up as you pleased. You don't get shops like that today.'

No, Midge thought, shrugging off the whispers and the shivers they'd induced, you get supermarkets. She retreated to the doorway, waited there, hoping he would notice that he was talking to himself and take the hint. He didn't. He was facing the other way, still reminiscing.

' – so many parcels and packages on the counter you could barely glimpse the postmistress. Mrs. Ritter, her name was. Little lady, but tough. The lads used to see what they could get away with and if she was in a good mood she might give them a quarter of boiled sweets or some licorice, but she'd clip 'em round the ear if she – '

Midge switched off. If he was going to give a detailed account of who once did what in every building in the village, even the *ruined* ones, she'd end up screaming, she knew she would. She heard him chuckle at another memory, groaned as he described the post coming on a cart from Wareham, wherever that was, and the postman passing the day before the afternoon collection on his allotment, or fishing.

Well, let him fish.

She stepped outside and watched people stroll by in small groups, pairs, singly. The singles passed by in worlds of their own. Lucky them, she thought, setting her back against the wall. Behind her the old man's voice continued to rumble along like the postman's cart. Closing her eyes against the day, the light, the people, her mind drifted, and almost at once she might have been anywhere, any other place or time, where parents stayed home, people took notice of her, and she was beautiful. The daydream was shattered by the sound of giant feet crushing brittle leaves in the shell of a building that she leant against. Juby's voice had ceased to rumble; he was on his way out. Rather than fall in with him again so soon, she pushed herself from the wall and darted away, weaving around and between camera-toting strollers.

At the end of the row, a short path through a shady dell delivered her to a dirt roadway that swung between the last cottage and the elevated churchyard opposite. A little way along, to her left, stood a small gabled building with a recently-tiled roof and red-painted window frames, but some distance beyond this, amid trees, she spotted a collapsed house, then another, and then half a wall of one more. What's with all the ruins? she wondered, while telling herself that it was nothing to her.

She crossed the road to the churchyard steps but did not climb them, choosing instead to stand nearby, in the shade of an old oak before which a large stone set in the ground informed her that the tree had been planted in 1911 to commemorate the coronation of King George V. Fascinating, she thought, unfascinated. From the tree she could see the entire ruined row of cottages, and Juby emerging from the third of them. Must be looking for her, she decided. Wondering where she'd got to. She watched him go into the last cottage. He remained inside for two or three minutes before coming out and entering the grove through which she'd preceded him. Seconds later, without any sign that he was seeking her, he was loping across the pebbled road toward her, mopping his brow with a handkerchief the size of a tea-towel. So he must have spotted her back there.

Known where she'd gone, just taken his own sweet time to get to her.

'What's up?' he asked as he reached the shade of the oak.

'Up?'

'You look puzzled.'

'I was wondering where the village is,' she replied.

'You're in it,' he said.

'No, the proper village, the part that's not ruined.'

'It's all ruined.'

'Uh?'

'Except the church, and the schoolhouse there. They've been restored, renovated, whatever you want to call it – for show, like the pond,' he added, stuffing the handkerchief back in his pocket and setting a shoulder against the trunk of the tree. 'Place's been deserted since the war, I thought everyone knew that.'

'Which war?'

He looked at her as if she were an imbecile. 'Which war do you think, the Boer War, the Hundred Years War, the Wars of the Roses?' His tone was sharp, his gray eyes cold.

'Well, there are always wars,' she said. 'It's hard to keep up sometimes.'

Juby slipped his hands in his trouser pockets, turned his loose change around, and nodded slowly, as if reluctantly conceding that the girl had a point.

'The last *world* war,' he said.

'Oh. Right. So, was it... bombed or something?'

'Bombed?' He laughed. 'Bombed, she says.' The laugh died. 'Hasn't Inger told you about Rouklye?'

'All she said was that it's where you and Grandpa used to live.'

'She didn't say that they turfed us out?'

'Turfed you out? Out of what? Who?'

'Who?'

'Turfed you out.'

'The government,' he said.

'The government?'

'Churchill's mob.' Catching her puzzled look, he said: 'You have heard of Churchill?'

'Yes. We covered him in school.'

'Covered him in school!' Juby sneered. 'Covered him in glory, too, I expect.'

'Well, he is a national hero, isn't he?'

Another laugh, a sharp bark of one, with no humor whatsoever. 'National hero! Do national heroes sign off on the eviction of over two hundred and twenty men, women and children from the homes they've lived in all their lives – for generations, in the case of some families?'

'I don't know about anything like that,' Midge said.

'Course you don't, why would you? Stuff like that won't be in your school history books. All right then, here it is. At the end of November 1943 everyone in Rouklye – the village, the entire valley right down to the coast – was given notice to quit. They had twenty-eight days to get out because it'd been decided – "decided!" – that the land could be put to better use by the Army, it being a time of war and all, but not to worry, they said, not to worry, you can come back when the war's over.' He looked away. 'It didn't happen.'

'Didn't happen?' Midge said.

'The Army's boots were too far under the table by the war's end. Didn't want to give it up, and they didn't, ever. Everything you see here today and a lot more that you don't, is still theirs, fifty-four years after the end of their goddam war.'

Midge glanced about her at individuals and families wandering wherever they wished, sitting on walls, taking pictures, kids squealing off in all directions.

'But all these people...'

'It's August,' Juby said.

'So?'

'The one month of the year the public's allowed in.' He snorted. 'The public! Day-trippers picking through our old homes in their nice summer clothes, taking home picture postcards from the church of what it used to be like. They have no idea, girl, no bloody idea.'

With this he stormed off.

Midge hesitated for perhaps a quarter of a minute, but then followed, slowly, looking around her at the derelict buildings and all that their dereliction now suggested, with just a little more interest than before.

6

Following Juby into the building he'd said was once the village school, she stood in a narrow vestibule with coat pegs on either side. Each peg had a small card by it with the name of a pupil who'd once attended the school. Her eye was caught by one of the names: Violent Croke. She gaped – *Violent Croke?!* – but closer inspection revealed that there was no 'n'.

She read the rest of the names without adding letters: Dorothy Ferris, Walter Richards, Kathleen Richards, Henry Braine, Vera Bellman, Tommy Ochart, Elizabeth Fannon, John Miller, Lizzie Naylor, Fred Day, a number of others. Above the pegs on one wall hung a framed photograph, cracked and brown with age, showing the children, aged from about four to fourteen, to whom the pegs belonged during their years in attendance at the school. A youngish schoolmistress, unsmiling, stood to one side of them, hands folded in front of her. Midge counted twenty-two pegs and twenty-two names, but thirty-one children in the picture, which suggested that there were either more pegs originally or that eight of the kids in the photo did without or doubled up. In the middle of the front row young Billy Brooker, who looked as if he'd been told to sit up straight and didn't want to, held a small writing slate on which the teacher had chalked 'Rouklye School 1912'. A typed note beside the photo stated that this same Billy Brooker was later drowned, aged fifteen, in a boating accident in Crowbarrow Bay.

The school itself was a single, heavily-beamed, chapel-like room. A pair of oil lamps dangled on long chains from the whitewashed ceiling. There was a brick fireplace with an old wood stove, and a series of linked desks with fixed benches. Samples of the work of former pupils were laid out on the desks, under glass like museum exhibits.

'Any of this yours?' Midge asked Juby, who was looking at other things in another parts of the room.

'Long before my day,' he said. 'Didn't go to school here anyway.'

A large blackboard stood on an easel to one side of the fireplace. The board's main headings were painted on. The rest, changed daily this month if no other, were neatly hand-written in chalk.

Welcome to Rouklye School
15th August

Weather Outlook

Sunny, hot, cooling sea breeze

Max 29c

Juby stepped up onto a slightly-raised platform at the far end of the room, squeezed himself onto the bench fixed to one side of a large desk that stood there, and stuck his chin on a fist to gaze out of the broad end window. He's an odd one, Midge thought. The way he looks, speaks, behaves. Even his name was odd. 'Juby Bench' was certainly on a par with 'Violet Croke' without the 'n'.

A small giggle behind her. She turned to see who'd come in. No one had. For the second time in less than twenty minutes her spine tingled, but when she saw a young family passing beyond the window she decided that one of the children must have briefly looked in.

To pass the time until Juby deigned to head on out, she strolled along the desks examining the work under glass. There were crayon and pencil drawings, childish poems about nature, weather, home life. There were also sums, spelling tests, things about religion, and 'lines'. The work didn't seem all that old-fashioned, and she found it hard to imagine that the kids who'd produced it would be very old now – those who were still about at all. Most would be long dead, like Billy Brooker. It wasn't so easy to be amused by their school work, or their names, when you remembered that.

Nearing the fireplace, she extended her fingers to the unlit fire, imagining the warmth of a good blaze on a freezing winter's day, then moved along to the piano, an old upright. Tempted to sit down and plink-plank-plunk a bit, a glance at Juby, preoccupied by the window, dissuaded her. Instead, she went to a display case that offered a selection of hand-written entries from the school register, which seemed to have doubled as a diary.

> *July 13th, 1911 Not so good an attendance this week. Children are kept away while mothers carry food to the hayfield.*

> *May 24th, 1912 Ernest Mawer has been away all week with a swollen face. Irene Day has been away since Wednesday owing to sickness.*

> *Aug. 2nd, 1912 Irene Day leaves today being 14 years of age next week. I am rather sorry to lose my older children.*

> *Oct. 26th, 1913 Attendance again lowered by the absence of Tommy Ochart who has not been to school since the holiday owing to having no boots.*

'Show you my house if you like.'

She glanced toward the platform at the end of the room. Juby's hulking silhouette at the desk.

'Your houssss…?'

The word skidded to a halt. There were two silhouettes at the desk, the second sitting across from Juby: a boy, thin and rangy, no less wild-haired than the man. She tried to speak, but her tongue refused to let go of the roof of her mouth.

A sudden cacophony behind her caused her to spin round as half-a-dozen kids burst in, followed by a quartet of adults. The adults clustered in the doorway, peering about without quite entering, while their less inhibited progeny threw themselves on the desks, laughing, squealing, shouting – 'Miss! Miss! Please, Miss!' – and sticking their hands in the air to attract an invisible teacher's attention.

An angry growl from the far end. Midge turned to see Juby jump to his feet. The other figure – the boy – was gone. Juby charged through the room, head down like a bull intent on getting out of the china shop come what may. She stepped smartly aside, as did the people crowding the doorway, and followed him at a more temperate pace, mumbling apologies to the parents.

The light outside was so blinding that she couldn't see him at first, but when she managed to make him out she forgot to breathe for several seconds. He stood against the churchyard wall opposite, in the shade of an elderly horse-chestnut, the sun, pouring through a break in the foliage, bleaching him away almost to nothing – then to nothing at all. For a fleeting moment it was as if he wasn't there. Didn't even exist. But then he was back again, and looking her way, as if waiting for her to join him.

That night she would describe this scene in the first of several proposed letters to Nessa Friedman, intending to mail them just before Ness returned from holiday. She would make no mention of the boy sitting across from Juby in the schoolroom – an illusion too ludicrous for words, even to her best friend.

Juby stepped out from the tree and led the way down a steep, narrow path to the building he wanted to show her. Unlike the cottages and most of the other buildings he would point out before he was done, this one still had its upper story, though its roof had either caved in or been removed. A mass of trees surrounded it, along with a cordon of high, dense weeds that tangled through and around barbed-wire and signs warning visitors to proceed no further for safety's sake. All that Midge could see of the house was the top portion of two upper windows, just the frames, no glass, and the crest of a gable end. Juby, being so tall, was not similarly disadvantaged. For a minute he simply stood there, gazing at the house, his back to her, and then she heard his voice. He wasn't speaking loudly, was just talking, as if to someone standing next to him, which she was not. She moved closer, listening, catching what she could.

'...knew nothing of the world outside, only... and that I was alive... nature all about... trees, birds, all kinds... summer mornings, open windows... cool breeze blowing through the valley, straight off the bay...'

Standing some little way behind him, it sounded to her as if he were reciting something either memorized or said before more than once, to someone or to himself, and when he'd finished, he turned, in 'duty-done' sort of way, and off he went again, and again she followed.

7

Inger and Edwin's house was seventeenth century, but not nearly as attractive or historically interesting as those two words imply. A good century and a half past its best, it was all rather wonky, inside and out, with sagging ceilings, banging pipes that regularly froze in winter, and tiles that popped off the roof when starlings landed.

The bookshop took up most of the ground floor, though the stone-flagged kitchen was a fair size, and, off the short corridor between the two, there was the former pantry that served as Inger's office. When there were browsers in the shop she would retreat to this cubbyhole so as not to put them off, but a hatch between the two allowed her to respond to enquiries or calls for service – and to keep an eye out for shoplifters. There was no one in the shop, customer or thief, the morning after the trip to Rouklye, but Inger was in the office anyway, 'Cooking the books,' she said when Midge brought her a mug of black coffee and a couple of digestives, adding, a moment or two later, 'Oh, Midge, a friend has invited you to visit her children this afternoon.'

'Her children?'

'The little Barstows. I've said you'll go, hope it's all right, if nothing else a visit to them will give you something to be grateful for.'

'Grateful?'

'That you don't live there.'

The Barstows lived some minutes' walk away, just outside the village and up a bit of hill. Edwin, assigned the task of escorting her there, donned the shapeless cricket hat that he'd never played cricket in, muttering, as they started out, 'Cruel woman, that, so cruel.'

'Who?' Midge asked.

'The Valkyrie, who else? I wouldn't have inflicted the Brat on you.'

'The Brat?'

'The second Barstow male. Every time I have the misfortune to be within reach of him, my hands twitch with longing to encircle his scrawny little neck. What did you make of Rouklye?'

Startled by the abrupt change of subject, her step faltered. 'It was... different,' she said.

'Your gran says Juby gave you the Tour. What did he say about the place?'

'Oh, you know...'

'I might. But tell me anyway.'

'He told me about everyone having to clear out way back...'

'During the war, yes. Anything else?'

'Um... he showed me a pane of glass he broke in the phone kiosk when he was fifteen.'

Edwin laughed. 'Did he now? That says a lot.'

'What do you mean?'

'Well, a dozen or so years ago Rouklye was used as the setting for a film about a bunch of 19th century laborers striking for better wages and conditions. It was the only village the film people could find that wasn't spoilt by time. Ruined, yes, but not spoilt, on account of its not having been lived in for over four decades. Many of the buildings had to be tarted up for the cameras, and by the time they'd put false fronts and thatched roofs on some of the cottages, a square tower on the church, everything looked perfect. I came along to take a gander. A lot of folk did. Pretty impressive.'

'And the telephone kiosk? Midge said.

'It wasn't shown in the film – wrong century – but there was a bad storm one night, terrible gale in off the sea, and some of the film-makers' scaffolding came down on it. Crunched it so badly that they had to replace it. So whoever cracked that pane of glass, it wasn't Juby Bench.'

'Maybe he doesn't know about the storm,' she said.

'Maybe a lot of things, Midge. Maybe a lot of things.'

A few paces further Edwin dropped his voice to a virtual whisper even though there was no one else about.

'Word to the wise,' he said. 'If the man of the house is at home don't mention Rouklye. His granddad helped supervise the '43 evacuation and Wystan gets a mite prickly if he hears anything against the takeover. Guilty conscience, I reckon, but don't quote me.'

He stopped before a moderately imposing Georgian house, and, of course, Midge stopped with him. As they did so, a woman rose from a large shrub beside the driveway.

'Ah. Our visitors.'

'Just the one,' Edwin said. 'I'm not stopping. Wild horses wouldn't make me, so don't try and persuade me. Midge, Mrs. Barstow, Mrs. Barstow, Midge.'

She was short and pleasantly plump, with a lively face, ash blonde hair curling around a lime-green headscarf as if by design. She dropped her pruning shears, removed one of her gardening gloves, extended the hand it had contained.

'Jilly. Pleased to meet you, Midge. I've heard so much about you.'

'She's heard nothing,' Edwin said out of the side of his mouth.

'Nat and Henry are looking forward to meeting you too,' Jilly said. 'Between ourselves, I think the holidays are dragging a bit. You'll be a nice distraction for them.'

Great, Midge thought. I'm not a person, I'm a distraction to entertain the lousy kids. And both boys too. It got worse by the minute.

The lady stepped back, drawing her by the hand she was still holding. 'You can go now,' she said to Edwin.

He looked grateful for this. 'Luck, Midge,' he said, and, as Humphrey Bogart: 'You're gonna need it, kid.' Switching to Charlie Chaplin, he headed homeward whirling an invisible cane, one foot on the curb, one in the gutter.

To Midge's partial relief it turned out that Henry was short for Henrietta. She was eight, and petite and sweet where her older brother, at fourteen – though he behaved two years younger – was neither. Nathaniel Barstow was extremely thin and pallid, with fair hair that flopped over one eye and a lip that curled when his mother introduced him to Midge.

'Nat, why don't you show Midge your room?'

The eye not concealed by hair narrowed suspiciously. 'What for?'

'Because she'd like to see it – wouldn't you, Midge?'

No, Midge thought, but made a passionless 'mmm' sound.

'Don't want to,' said Nat the Brat sulkily.

'Come on now, darling. Midge is our guest.'

He grunted, and turned; stomped upstairs.

'He's shy,' Jilly said with slightly strained brightness. 'He's very proud of his room. You go on after him, Midge, while I squeeze us some lemon squash.'

Midge glanced at Henrietta, kneeling on the floor weaving model cars in and out of an obstacle course of tins and cereal packets. Henry caught her glance. 'You can play with me,' she offered.

'I'd rather,' she whispered, but the choice wasn't hers to make. She went upstairs. On the square landing at the top she was faced with several closed doors. 'Hello?'

When there was no reply she knocked on the nearest.

Again no response, so she rapped on each of the others in turn, wishing she could go back down. Even toy cars and cereal boxes with an eight year old would have the edge on this.

It was the last door that turned out to front the room she was obliged to seek, identified by a wordless shout that was anything but welcoming. She bridled – who did the little creep think he was? – and spun around, headed for the stairs. But a second before she started down, Nathaniel's door flew back. She glanced toward it. He stood in the doorway, no longer wearing jeans and T-shirt but camouflage trousers and matching jacket.

'Thought you wanted to see my room,' he said.

'No idea where you got that from,' she answered.

'Come on then,' he said.

She opened her mouth to say something unpleasant, but instead sighed, and returned. He stood to attention, holding the door open for her, and she walked past him, into his room – and reared back in amazement.

The walls of Nathaniel Barstow's room were covered with posters, prints and photographs depicting air battles, land battles, sea battles, in which guns blazed, bombs exploded, and depth charges sped toward underwater targets. There were infantrymen with fixed bayonets belting hell-for-leather across deformed landscapes; men sprawling on smoke-shrouded battlefields; soldiers leaping from trenches, torn apart by mortar shells. But the pictures were only the half of it. Every space and surface was crammed with small replicas of machines of war, and there was a battle game on the floor with armies ranged against one another. Even the duvet depicted a scene of conflict. There were guns of various kinds too, and hand-grenades. The guns didn't look quite real, but the grenades did.

On the wall behind the bed, an enormous map of the world was covered with curved red arrows suggesting points of attack or troop movement, along with a multitude of colored pins. One of the pins was situated very near where she thought her parents were right now. To think, they were all the way out there in the South Pacific trying to stop some military dictatorship testing weapons that could kill thousands – millions perhaps – and here was she, their only child, being given a private view of this little twit's war room.

'Bet you never saw a room like this before,' Nathaniel said proudly.

'Not in this lifetime,' she replied.

'I'm gonna join the Army when I'm old enough.'

'Really.'

'My dad says I can start training to be an officer soon as I leave school. I'm gonna be a gen – '

The crunch of wheels on gravel cut him short. Nathaniel leapt onto the window seat and leant out. 'Dad!' he yelled. 'Dad!'

Midge also looked out. A man in the uniform of an Army officer was getting out of a gleaming black Saab. He looked up and waved. Nat the Brat's role model was home.

8

Major Wystan Barstow unbuttoned his collar and tugged his tie loose as he strolled through the house, stepped over Henry and her cars, and out onto the patio.

'This heat!'

He slipped his jacket off, slung it over one of the green garden chairs, and sank gratefully into the lounger his wife had been using earlier to enhance her already glowing tan.

'Lemon squash, darling?'

'Lemon squash? You have to be joking.'

Jilly went inside and Wystan closed his eyes, let his jaw go slack. Peace. Until the rifle barrel plunged into his mouth.

'You're dead meat,' growled his son and heir.

Barstow senior's eyes flew open. 'Unnggh?'

The young soldier standing over him, finger on trigger, leered triumphantly, but his father wasn't an officer for nothing. Deftly removing the barrel from his mouth, he rolled off the lounger and wrestled the boy to the ground.

Obliged to shadow him until she received new orders, Midge had followed Nathaniel out. She winced at his thin voice, his bellows and threats as he fought his father, longing to be anywhere but here.

'Wystan, this is Inger and Edwin's granddaughter, Midge.'

Major Barstow froze. He looked up, disconcerted to find a stranger watching him wrestling with his son on the ground. Nat continued to flail, but his father said something to him which, after repeating it more sharply, caused him to lie still.

Wystan got to his feet and pulled the knot of his tie from under his left ear, a lopsided grin forming beneath his dark moustache. He proffered Midge his hand.

'Hi. Visiting with the oldies then, are you?'

'While her parents are away,' Jilly answered for her, 'on... business.'

The last word was so loaded that her husband couldn't fail to miss it. Then he recalled the many reports of the campaigning Millers and their crackpot organization's mission to save the world from itself. He withdrew his hand, which Jilly put a can of cold beer into. He punctured the can, gulped at it, and kept on gulping as though it were his first drink for days.

'Midge?'

The promised lemon squash, in a tall slim tumbler. 'Thanks.' She took it and sipped. It was good. So good that she drained half the glass before she could bear to lower it, understanding very well how the officer of the house felt about his cold beer.

'Dad! Let's fight some more!'

'Not now, Nat, too hot. And we have a visitor.'

Nathaniel was not pleased. 'I want to *fight*!' he snarled.

'Yeah, well I don't, all right? Now don't have one of your fits. Go and cool off in the fish pond or something.'

Nathaniel's eyes were furious slits as his father sank back onto the lounger. Midge glanced at Henry, who'd come out when her brother started playing up. Young as she was, Henry knew him all too well. Knew that he wasn't one to stroll off quietly when told. She watched him turn about and stalk away, then touched Midge's arm.

'Show you my room now?'

'Midge might not want to see your room, dear,' Jilly said, plucking her husband's jacket from the chair and folding it over her arm, smoothing creases with the flat of her hand.

'I don't mind,' Midge said.

Henry gripped her wrist and tugged her toward the house, but a sharp yell from down the garden skidded her to a halt.

'Nat?' said Jilly in alarm.

She dropped Wystan's jacket and hurried away to rescue her son from whatever hideous fate threatened him. Wystan closed his eyes. 'That boy,' he muttered, but when another distant cry reached him he sighed, eased himself out of the lounger, and went wearily after his wife.

'Natty playing silly buggers,' Henry said to Midge.

When the trio returned Wystan was furious, Jilly was upset, and Nathaniel was drenched from head to foot.

'Sometimes, boy,' his father was saying, 'I have serious doubts about your sanity. When I say cool off in the fish pond I'm joking, right? You know what a joke is? God, I should have stayed on base. I'm going up to get changed.'

While her husband marched into the house, Jilly dropped to her knees to remove her son's Army boots. When they were off, she led him inside, casting a slightly embarrassed smile Midge's way in passing.

9

She was dreaming of the old cottages, but in the dream the weeds and ivy were gone and they had roofs and doors, and windows with curtains. Every dwelling looked habitable yet there was no one about, until, in the distance, a figure – a boy – walked round a corner. Seeing her, he stopped. Stared back at her. He being too far off for her to get a good look at him, she might have started toward him, but then – *rap-rap-rap* – and the door opened, and Inger said: 'Midge, dear, sorry to wake you, email from your mum. Trish printed it out for me. Just as well it's one of her days, I have no patience with this emaily stuff.'

She sat up, fast, the dream behind her.

'Email? My mother never sends emails. What's up? What's wrong?'

Inger approached, handed her the sheet of paper. 'Don't panic, just a communication to keep us up to date.'

She left the room and Midge read the email.

> Inanians proving difficult but we'll spoil their
> fun if they don't blast us out of the water first.
> Hope all's well there, love Kris and Dave.

She'd barely finished reading it for the third time when Inger returned. 'Oh, Midge, do you think you could avoid using the khazi for a while?'

'The what?'

'Edwin's word. The lav. Toilet. It's blocked. Happens all the time. Victorian plumbing. Shouldn't be for too long. I've called a man to fix it, name of Rainey.'

The door closed. Midge read the email one more time, then got out of bed and cast about for somewhere to lodge it. Her mother sometimes stuck postcards and other small printed items in the corners of picture frames. Well, plenty of those here. She folded the sheet of paper and was slotting the message into one of the thin black frames on the wall when she noticed that the picture it contained was of the row of cottages she'd walked among two days earlier, except that in the picture they weren't ruined. Her dream came back to her. She'd dreamt of them as they looked here, with upper floors and roofs, smoke lazing out of chimneys, small gardens that ended at the gated wall, by the telephone kiosk.

A horse and cart stood outside the wall, and there were women and girls in long skirts, a couple of men in bowler hats, hands in pockets, loitering for the camera. At the bottom of the picture, handwritten in faded brown ink, was a caption: 'Post Office Row'.

She looked at the next picture along: Rouklye church viewed from below the steps where she'd waited for Juby. Unlike the cottages, the church in the photo looked much the same in the present day, but the third picture – of a massive vine-covered house standing four-square in well-tended grounds bound by a high brick wall – was another story entirely. According to the writing underneath, this was the rectory. The rectory Juby had shown her was a gray husk of a building that ended abruptly where the first floor had once begun. The broad doors were gone, the enormous windows reduced to empty rectangles, the walls of the great rooms stripped back to bare stone, while the neat paths and fine gardens had become a featureless tract of open ground without a single flower, bush or shrub.

She glided along to the next picture, and the next, the next, all down the line, straightening them as she went without thinking. Some showed bits of countryside she hadn't seen, or a stretch of coast, but most were of houses and cottages that were either ruined now or no longer existed in any form. Every property had a name, or the names of the people who were living there when the picture was taken, written on small rectangles of yellowing card, occasionally with a scrap of information about them. She discovered, for instance, that Stile Cottage had stood above a place called Thorn Hollow, that a family by the name of Warren had lived there for a time, and that Cowleaze, a bungalow, had been built in 1910 by the Mulliner family for use as a summer residence. And there was Brooker's Thatch. No information about this one, but could it be the home of Billy Brooker, whose picture she'd seen above the pegs in the schoolhouse? The Billy Brooker who drowned at the age of fifteen?

The last two photos were of a more imposing property than any but the rectory. The captions below both of these read 'Rouklye Great House'. In the garden of one, a girl of seven or eight stood in a white pinafore dress holding a tennis racquet. Midge wondered who she was and how she'd ended up. Was she still alive, an old biddy in a wheelchair eking out a pension in some anonymous bungalow, constantly comparing life today with how it used to be, at the Great House when she was young? Midge recalled her contempt for these photos, and was just a little bit ashamed. Turning from the last picture, she caught the Midge in the mirror, also turning, and could not meet her eye.

Stepping out of range of the mirror, she bumped into the little table containing the wooden chess set. Several of the pieces toppled over. She knew nothing about chess, but putting the pieces back on the right squares was a simple matter of copying the arrangement of the opposing pieces.

Like the photos on the wall and the bits of crude rock dotted about the room, she hadn't given the chess set more than a cursory glance before, but now that she looked at it properly she realized how fine it was, in a hand-carved sort of way. It was made from two kinds of wood, half the squares and one set of pieces being fairly light in color, the rest as black as jet. The whole thing needed dusting. She wiped one of the chessmen with a tissue. It glowed gratefully. She considered polishing the rest, but decided there wasn't much point as it wasn't a complete set. She wondered where the missing piece had got to. One of the black corner pieces with battlements on top.

She got dressed and opened the door to go down to breakfast just as Edwin came strolling along the landing in blue rubber gloves, carrying a large plunger.

'Crapper,' he said as he went by.

'Pardon me?'

'Tommy Crapper. Made Queen Victoria's first flushing throne. This one too. Haven't you noticed his logo on the pan?' He entered the smallest room at the end of the landing. 'Funny the things people choose to invent, isn't it?' he said over his shoulder. 'I mean Mr. C might have pioneered the motor car, the deckchair, a range of sweets, anything at all. You can see it, can't you? Crapper's Jelly Babies. Crap sweets for short.'

He got down on his knees in front of the large white bowl and inserted the plunger.

'But no,' he went on. 'He wakes up one day and says to himself, "I know, I'll go into flush toilets!" Just as well really, or who knows what I'd have been doing to pass the time this fine morning. You know, Midge,' he added as she was about to go downstairs, 'I sometimes wonder if I took a wrong turn in my youth. Had a fancy to sail the seven seas, be a dashing adventurer, great lover of tall women. Instead I became a ledger clerk, barely looked up from a desk for forty-five years, and here I am today, henpecked, pensioned off, arm down a U-bend. You have to laugh.'

Hoping he wouldn't be in there all day, Midge descended the narrow staircase, into a pall of black smoke.

Inger was happy to admit to anyone who cared that she was no cook. The preparation of meals, she'd decided long ago, was what the Edwins of this world were for. She could rustle up a fair breakfast cereal when pressed, but her culinary expertise ended there. Toast was a particular problem for her. The trouble with toast was that it had a selfish way of burning itself to a crisp while she stood gazing out of the window or leaning on the table browsing through *The Times*. Fortunately, she preferred her toast a little on the dark side; fine for her if rather less so for those with more delicate palates and a full set of working nostrils.

Midge's eyes smarted as she spluttered through the swirling smog and reached for the packet of Bran Flakes; tipped some into a bowl. Inger drew her attention to the row of charred relics in the toast rack.

'I've scraped a couple specially for you.'

'No thanks.'

'Muesli then?'

'This is fine.' She opened the fridge door. 'Any milk?'

'Last drop went in my tea, sorry. Not sure if today's has been delivered yet. That milkman, he turns up whenever he pleases.'

'I'll go look.'

She went out to the step, and gulped gratefully at the clean air. The milk was there, two bottles, the caps already delved into by birds. A printed note was tucked between them, not from the birds.

> It is regretted that due to falling demand and
> increased costs, bottled milk will no longer be
> delivered from Sept 13. From that date milk will
> be delivered in cartons at a slightly revised price,
> about which customers will be notified shortly.

She folded the note, picked up the bottles.

'Morning, Evy! What's happening over there on the sunny side of the street?'

Juby Bench, leaning out of his window at The Ferryman. She glanced up and down the street. No one about, but there were houses on both sides, and people in them, with ears. She held the bottles up, hoping that would be a sufficient response.

'Had your brekkies?' Juby bawled back.

'Just going to!' A shouted whisper as she edged toward the door.

'They do a good breakfast here! Keep you going all day, breakfasts at The Ferryman! Why don't you join me?'

She considered pretending that she hadn't heard this and rushing back indoors, but –

'Yeah, good idea! Come over! And bring the old girl! Inger! I'll just get into me pants and put a comb through me hair! Fifteen minutes, dining room, see you there!'

He ducked inside and Midge went back into the house wishing she hadn't gone for the milk.

The windows were open in the kitchen, but it was another still day and the air wasn't in a wafting mood. Inger now sat at the epicenter of the fog spreading *Mackay's Dundee Orange Marmalade* on buttered black toast while reading the paper. When Midge dropped the dairy's note on the table, she read it with disdain.

'It had to happen. Pity. I like my bottles, even if the blasted birds do get to them first. And "slightly revised price"! We know what *that* means, don't we? We'll be paying more for dreadful little cardboard boxes that can't be opened without milk sloshing everywhere.'

She screwed up the note and tossed it over her shoulder.

'I just saw Juby,' Midge said. 'He invited us over for breakfast.'

'I heard. All Underthorpe heard. I'm already having

mine.' A finger and thumb dropped the corner of toast and she gulped at a mug of tea. 'You go. I'll try and make it another time, tell him.'

'I can't go on my own!'

Inger looked up. Smiled at her with charcoaled teeth.

'Course you can. Juby's not an ogre. He just looks like one.'

10

Inside The Ferryman, behind a high oak counter that gleamed with polished age, a young woman in a neat white blouse looked up from the staff rota she was examining.

'Help you?'

'I'm here to see Mr. Bench,' Midge said. When the receptionist's blank expression suggested a need for further information, she added, 'He told me to come over for breakfast.'

'Oh, you're visiting a resident. What name again?'

'Mr. Bench. Juby Bench.'

'Bench...' The woman ran a finger down the register. 'My first morning back from holiday, not sure who's... Ah! J.S. Bench.' She looked up. 'You're sure he's expecting you?'

'Yes.'

'I'll ring through to his room, tell him you're here.'

A small panic. 'No, it's all right, I'll wait, he said the dining room, fifteen minutes, it must be about that.'

'He probably meant the Breakfast Room.' The receptionist pointed through a lofty archway, beyond which Midge could see square tables covered in white cloths. 'If you wait there, Mr. Rackham will look after you.'

She crossed the floral-carpeted hall, wishing Juby hadn't invited her. The kitchen smog would have been preferable to this place, with its musty smell, its red flock wallpaper, the antlered head staring from the wall. She felt silly here. Helpless. Completely out of place.

'Evy!'

She jumped; glanced toward the broad staircase to her right: Juby, in his black suit, which looked so rumpled today that he might have slept in it.

'Where's Inger?' he asked as he joined her.

'She was already eating. Said another time.'

'Come on then, let's you and me go and pad ourselves out a bit.'

He strode into the Breakfast Room and she followed. It wasn't a large room. There were just eight tables, two of which were occupied by couples, one quite elderly, reading newspapers while they ate, the other in their early-20s, grinning at one another as Mr. Rackham, the proprietor, finished serving them.

'Morning, Reg,' Juby said. 'Table for two today. Have you met my guest? Miss Evy Miller, Inger and Ed's granddaughter.'

'How-de-do,' Mr. Rackham said with a small bow, and, to Juby: 'Where would you like to sit?'

'The window, as usual.'

They went to the window table, where Midge was about to seat herself when she felt the chair being eased in beneath her from behind, and half rode on it, the thick tablecloth brushing her legs. Juby seated himself across from her, without assistance. Then they were each handed a small menu card.

'Leave you for a minute?' Mr. Rackham asked.

'A minute should do it,' said Juby.

Midge settled her elbows on the table so that the little menu was on a level with her eyes, and peeped over it at her host, pondering his own menu. It wasn't only his suit that was rumpled this morning. His face was corrugated with lines, he hadn't shaved, and if he'd combed his hair as he said he was going to it hadn't made much difference. The hair she could sympathize with. The only time hers looked reasonable was when she was climbing out of the chair at the hairdresser's. Almost always, in the street thirty seconds later, it was all over the place again.

'Dunno why I look at this,' Juby said, dropping the menu. 'Always have the Full English at The Ferryman. The *child's* Full English here is like the adult's in most places. Not that I'm suggesting you have the child's, of course.'

She glanced at the component parts of the Full English

Breakfast (adult's) and gasped.

'I can't eat this much!'

'Sure you can.'

'And I've never had fried bread.'

'Never had fried bread? Everybody's had fried bread.'

'I haven't. And...' – she hesitated, not wanting to sound fussy – 'I don't really like mushrooms.'

'No problem. All the rest though? Leave what you can't manage for Reg's cats.'

He inclined his head and Mr. Rackham came over. Juby ordered an extra sausage for Midge in place of the mushrooms, and for himself the standard Full English (adult's): bacon, sausage, egg, baked beans, mushrooms, tomato, fried bread.

'Come on,' he said when they were alone, 'let's get our starters.'

'Starters? As well?'

Juby laughed. 'I'm a growing lad, you're a growing gal!'

He shoved his chair back and Midge followed him to a large framed print – blue from years of exposure to direct sunlight – of a three-masted schooner in a storm. On a table below the picture there was an assortment of single-portion cereal packets and two glass jugs, one containing milk, the other orange juice. Juby poured them each a tumbler of orange and broke two boxes of cereal into an inadequate white bowl for himself. Midge also took a bowl, but contented herself with a single portion of *Frosties*. The milk jug was enormous and so full that it required both of her hands to lift it.

She followed Juby back to the table, trying not to spill the contents of her glass and bowl. Once they were seated, he plugged his face with a heaped spoonful and began to crunch noisily while she set about her cereal with an elegance that would have surprised her parents. Feeling far from right breakfasting with an old man in a hotel, she imagined that all eyes and thoughts must be on her. She glanced around. The young couple were too involved in one another to wonder about her, but the male half of the elderly pair was whispering to his wife, who smiled uncertainly at Midge. She turned to the bay window. There wasn't much of a garden beyond it, just a rectangle of crazy-paving within a sun-beaten border of stunted flowers, and two large black bins. The lid of one of the bins had fallen off and lay upside down on the ground. A ginger cat stood on the lid, tugging at a strip of bacon stuck to it.

While Juby crunched away, Midge decided that they had already run out of things to say to one another. If only Inger had been there. Then she wouldn't have felt a need to break the crunchy silence with inanities like...

'What you doing today then?'

He shrugged. 'Same as yesterday, same as the day before, tomorrow too, all being well.'

'Rouklye?'

'It's what I come over for.'

'But there's nothing there.'

'There's enough.' He polished off his cereal in two final mouthfuls. 'Thought I'd head out to Crowbarrow today. Get me some sea air.'

'Sea air?'

At once she was visualizing salt water on shingle, gulls wheeling overhead, sand between her toes.

'You like the sea, Evy?'

'Mm.'

'You can't come with me,' he said.

She look up at him. 'I didn't ask to.'

He sat back. 'No, that'd never do.'

She returned to her cereal. 'Things to do here anyway.'

He ruminated for a few moments, probing the gaps between his teeth with the tip of his tongue.

'Besides, I'm not only going to the sea. Be walking all over. Anywhere that's not restricted. That's what I do. I won't be rushing back.'

'Don't worry about it,' she said, chasing the last of the *Frosties* round her bowl.

Juby gazed at her bowed head, drooping shoulders, and, though she didn't see it, his expression softened.

'You know, you remind me of someone.'

She looked up. 'I do?'

'You do.'

'Who?'

'Not sure. The boy maybe.' Before she could ask what

boy, he said: 'You'll have to clear it with the grandparents.'

'Clear what with them?'

'You coming with me.'

'I thought I couldn't.'

'You want to or don't you?'

'Well,' she said.

'You'll be bored rigid.'

'I'm bored here.'

He considered some more, then said: 'Only if you get their say-so, though.'

'I'll ask Gran,' Midge said.

'Here we are then.'

This last was from Mr. Rackham, bearing two loaded plates. Midge gaped at the food mountain he set before her. 'Right after breakfast,' she said.

11

Juby's car was as worn and scruffy as its owner, but surprisingly comfortable. As they drove out of Underthorpe, Midge stretched up in the passenger seat to see if she could reach the roof with the top of her head. She couldn't, quite, unlike the driver, who was obliged to sit hunched over the wheel. Whenever they went over a bump there was a dull thud, followed by a small grunt, as his skull reintroduced itself to the roof. He never remarked on this. She had to ask.

'This car.'

'What about it?' Juby said.

'It's got a very low roof for a tall person.'

'Oh, I don't know.'

'You don't think you'd be better off with a bigger one?'

'Bigger car?'

'Yes. Then you could sit up straight.'

'I am sitting up straight.'

'No you're not.'

He glanced at each of his shoulders in turn, bunched up round his ears. 'You know, you're right. I never noticed.'

'How long have you had it?' Midge said. 'The car.'

'Oh, years. Almost from new.'

'You bought it almost from new and you didn't notice you had to crouch over the wheel to drive?'

'Can't say I did. Funny, that.'

It being early in the day, Rouklye car park wasn't nearly as crowded this time. They might have arrived sooner still if Inger hadn't insisted on making sandwiches for the pair of them and a flask of tea for Juby. 'I don't know what Edwin will say when he hears,' she said as she arranged the refreshments in a canvas shoulder bag.

'About what?' Midge asked.

'You going there with Juby again, and without me to keep his feet on the ground.'

When they got out of the car, the sun slapped them hard.

Midge scowled at the harsh light. Yet again she'd forgotten her sunglasses. Juby didn't wear sunglasses. He felt the heat, though, and threw his jacket across the back seat. Inger's insistence that her granddaughter coat her exposed parts with a sun block factor 30 had been a wise precaution. Juby obviously didn't bother with sun blocks of any factor. His skin looked as if it were made of the same old brown leather as his car seats – but when he fell against the vehicle on the driver's side he was instantly so ashen that even the leathery tan seemed to have drained away.

'What's up?' she asked.

'Nothing. Nothing. Got out of that crouch too fast.'

He gave it a moment more before reaching in for the refreshment bag, then slammed the door and strode away without locking it.

This time he headed not down to the village but in the opposite direction, toward the top end of the car park. The faded blue short-sleeved shirt he wore today wasn't much less rumpled than his saggy-bottomed trousers, and he still wore the sandals that had seen better days. Comparing their attire, Midge felt far too smart – and bright – in her crisp white top and cerise shorts.

'You know what?' Juby said, to himself apparently, for she was walking some way behind him. She sped up to catch the rest. 'They have a Conservation Officer who travels the country giving slide shows and lectures about the wonderful work the Ministry of Destruction does on the land it's stolen.

They even have their own magazine, praising their efforts in protecting wildlife, nature and all. And what do you think they call it? "Sanctuary". Sanctuary! If you ever want to know the meaning of the word hypocrisy, look no further.'

Glancing neither to right nor left as he walked, he failed to see a white Toyota sweep in from the road, but Midge did.

'Watch out!'

She grabbed his arm and pulled him to a halt. He stared at her hand, then her face.

'What?' he asked.

She released him and indicated the car, which had stopped inches from him. Juby glanced blankly at the Toyota, the scowling driver behind the windscreen, and walked on. Again Midge hurried after him. Caught up with him as he continued speaking as if there'd been no interruption.

'Wildlife preserve for centuries, this valley, before the uniforms moved in with their tanks and explosives, their barbed-wire and all. Wasn't called that, of course; it was just the way of things. Protecting nature? They wouldn't know nature if it flapped in their face and beaked their sodding eyes out. Nature means natural. Tell me what's natural about fencing species off from one another, human or animal.'

'But you keep coming back,' Midge said.

'Yes, I do, don't I?' Then he sighed. 'Well, never again. Last time, this.'

'Today, you mean?'

'Last trip. Ever. Look at that.'

His 'Look at that' was for the large noticeboard they'd come to at the edge of the car park.

YOU ARE NOT ALLOWED TO: -
TRADE, LIGHT FIRES,
STAY OVERNIGHT
OR CYCLE ON THE WALKS.
PLEASE TAKE YOUR LITTER HOME
AND KEEP DOGS UNDER CONTROL.
DO NOT USE METAL DETECTORS.
ENJOY THE WONDERFUL VIEWS.

'Or else,' Juby said, walking on.

Beyond the car park, woods enclosed by barbed-wire stretched far to the right and a little to the left, the two parts separated by a track just wide enough for a single vehicle, though a notice stated that no civilian transport was allowed there. Some way into the twin shadows of the divided wood the track became a bridge over a shallow brook. Juby paused here, and, naturally, Midge paused with him.

'Listen,' he said.

She did so. 'All I can hear is the water.'

'That's right.'

'So...?'

'Used to be a lot more than the sound of water here. Thick with birds, these woods were. All the Rouklye woods, all sorts of birds. Hear 'em all day long, from before dawn to past dark. And the rooks. I loved those birds. Their croaky old voices. Antisocial creatures, they say, but they like to be near farms, villages, people. That doesn't strike me as so antisocial, does it you?'

His gaze drifted among the upper branches of the silent trees.

'After we were given the push I sneaked back a few times and they were gone, every last one of them. Rooks here for centuries – that's where Rouklye got its name, they say – but I never saw nor heard a one from the day they kicked us out. You know, I always had this idea that if the rooks came back, if just one returned...'

She waited, but there was nothing more except, after a pause, a sharp sniff – the kind that puts a categorical end to sentimental notions – after which he withdrew his gaze from the birdless trees and continued across the bridge. As ever, she followed, like some incidental accessory.

At the end of the track a notice instructed visitors to keep within the yellow markers that bordered all paths and tracks. Near this a grey stone slab that greatly resembled a tombstone gave visitors a choice of direction: to the right Crowbarrow Bay, or ahead, over a cattle grid, a footpath through an overgrown meadow to a range of high cliffs.

'Four-hundred feet above sea level at their peak, those cliffs,' Juby said. 'When I was a lad I walked along them all the time, along 'em, down to the cove. Good weather, I'd strip off and have me a nice dip down there.'

'You won't be doing that today, will you?' she said.

He snorted. 'If I did they'd probably stand me against a rock and shoot me. This way.'

He started along the track to Crowbarrow. Again, she had to get a move on to keep up with him. She asked how far it was.

'A mile, give or take,' he said. 'No distance, kids like us.'

The sun beat down mercilessly from an opaque blue sky, uncluttered but for a smattering of white strands feathering across it. The fenced-off woods ran along the right-hand side of the track. Fixed to the fence, a notice, in capitals:

KEEP OUT

BOMBS AND UNEXPLODED

SHELLS IN HERE

THEY CAN KILL YOU

'They're joking, right?' Midge said.

'Oh yeah,' Juby said. 'Known for its jokes, the Army.'

To the left of the track a rising meadow became a long hill, near the top of which three armored tanks sat. The tanks weren't moving but as she and Juby walked it felt to her as if their great gun barrels might swivel at a moment's notice and blast her into the woods. Also on the hill stood a series of large black boards, each bearing a single red numeral:

4 5 6 7

'What are the numbers for?' she asked.

'You've heard of painting-by-numbers?' Juby said. 'Well round here they have blowing-up-hills-by-numbers.'

After some fifty yards, they heard a motor behind them and moved out of the way. A khaki-colored Land Rover with crimson stripes on the sides bumped by, kicking up dust and small stones.

'Range warden,' Juby hissed. 'Watch out. Authority.'

The Land Rover pulled to a halt a short way ahead of them and the driver jumped out and knelt to inspect a stretch of fencing that had come away. 'Another fine day,' he said as they drew level.

Juby grunted and stopped to watch him twist the wire with a pair of pliers. Midge loitered behind him. 'My young friend here,' Juby said to the man's back, 'was wondering if all the woods are out of bounds.'

'No, I wasn't,' she protested, but quietly.

The warden glanced round. 'They are,' he said to her. 'Some rare flowers in there.'

'Only flowers?' Juby said with exaggerated innocence.

The man straightened up, gave him an I-know-your-game look, and rattled about among his tools in the Land Rover. Then, hammer in hand, he again addressed Midge.

'Thousands of tank shells are fired on the range every year and there's always a few that don't go off. Some land in the sea, some on the hills, some in the woods. With the best will in the world we can't keep track of 'em all. The fences aren't there for decoration.'

She glanced apprehensively at the way ahead.

'Don't worry,' the warden said. 'All access points are swept for unexploded devices before the public's let in. You'll be fine as long as you don't go where you're not supposed to.'

He gave the fence post a couple of thumps with the hammer, tugged it this way and that to make sure it wouldn't move, and climbed back into his vehicle. Then, waving an arm out of the door, he sped off along the track.

Midge soon discovered that a mile is a long way for near strangers of very different generations to walk together. When the last of the chit-chat had dried up, they trudged in silence. Glad of any distraction, she was relieved when she heard a brisk footfall close behind. She looked round, ready to step aside to let whoever it was go by.

There was no one there.

Yet the footsteps continued, passed by, went on ahead of them.

She tried to speak, but could only gulp, repeatedly.

Juby, a few paces ahead, glanced back.

'What's up?'

'Did you hear that?' she managed in a tight little voice.

'Hear what?'

'F... footsteps.'

For a second she thought he was about to smile, but he

didn't, quite, or even pass comment, merely continued walking. Not wanting to be alone all of a sudden, she rushed after him.

In a minute, Juby said: 'Tell me about Miss Miller.'

'Miss Miller?'

'You.'

'There's nothing to tell.'

'There's always something to tell. You've got a home, haven't you? You have friends, interests, likes and dislikes. And you're not English.'

'Not English,' she said. 'I didn't think it showed.'

'You hide it well,' he said.

Ransacking her brain for something to say about herself that wasn't too personal, she ended up blurting a handful of self-conscious scraps that gave little away and sounded so dull that even she was bored.

'Your turn,' she said when she was done.

'My turn?'

'To tell me about you.'

'I wouldn't know where to start,' he said gruffly.

Keener to reverse their roles than actually learn more about him, she said: 'It doesn't matter where.'

He reflected for a few paces, before: 'Polynesian nose-flutes.'

'What?'

'I used to play them. For the rent, food, ciggies and so on. I smoked then. Rolled me own. I'm talking about the nineteen-fifties. That's how I met Inger. Busking. In Amsterdam.'

She gaped. 'You met my gran in Amsterdam? Busking?'

'There I was, playing my nose off on this street corner,' Juby said, 'and along comes this dark-haired beauty in shorts up to here, drops a few coppers in me cap, and we get to talking, she buys me a meal, and...'

He smiled, and left it at that.

'And that was her?' Midge said.

'She'd not long graduated from university in Oslo. On a solo walking tour to get all the work out of her system, she said. She was in no hurry, so she stuck around and I showed her how to play the nose-flutes.'

'Nose-flutes! You're making it up.'

'Making it up?' he said. 'I'll have you know I did very well with the flutes on the streets of Europe. Brussels, Paris, Berlin, wherever. Inger, though, she didn't really have the nose. Couldn't get the hang of breathing out with a pipe up each nostril. It's an art.'

'It'd have to be. What happened after you met?'

'Well, I'd been out of England for the best part of a decade, and it'd been on my mind to pop back and see how the old place was getting on without me, and as she wasn't working to a strict route or schedule she said she'd tag along. We hiked down through Holland, across Belgium, top end of France, and from there to Dover. A ferry helped with that bit.'

'A fairy?'

'A boat. For the water. Made a good team, Inger and me. We could keep pace with one another, had plenty to talk about, never fell out, and...'

He trailed off, back in the old days with lithe young Inger Bjølstad.

'Just good friends, I suppose,' Midge said.

He chuckled. 'It was a long walk.'

Thanks to the irregular lie of the land, no matter how far they went the sea never quite revealed itself, but when they'd walked about three quarters of the way Juby began pointing out where this or that dwelling once stood: beside the track, amid the trees, in that dip, up there in a fold of the hillside. Of most there remained nothing more than a ragged line of stones, or a door-frame supported by a bit of crumbling wall, while others had vanished entirely. He had a name for almost every building, whether there was anything left of it or not, a few of which she recalled from the captions on the photos in her room: Stile Cottage, Cutting Cottage, Chine House. Some of the names were not those of properties at all, but of individuals or families that had lived in them. Juby waved an arm in the direction of a line of tumbled stones.

'Brooker's Thatch,' he said. 'The "thatch" was because of the roof. Risky thing out here, thatch, the gales on this part of the coast.'

'Brooker's Thatch?' Midge said. 'Would that be where Billy Brooker lived?'

He glanced at her. 'Where'd you hear of Billy Brooker?'

'He was in a photo in the school room.'

'Billy was way before my time, but I remember his folks, and his sisters. The Brookers kept a few cows out here, a few more down in the village, near the rectory. Had a man take the milk round in pails, door to door, ladling it out by the pint. No milk bottles then.'

'None now either, soon,' she muttered.

'Now there's a sight for a day like this!' Juby said suddenly.

She'd been walking the final stretch sideways, picking out the tumbled stones of Brooker's Thatch, gazed at mere hours ago as a complete building in a thin black frame. Turning to see what Juby had referred to, she saw that the hill to their left had declined sharply into a dazzling blue expanse contained within the horseshoe of Crowbarrow Bay. Her eyes lit up. At last!

But then, a feeling to one side of her of having been joined by another. She turned. A ragged-haired youth stood a couple of yards away, gazing at the sea in a rapture that reflected her own of a moment before. Where had he sprung from? She looked harder. She'd seen him before, recently. A momentary turmoil while she tried to remember. Then she had it. The schoolroom, that first visit, the second silhouette, sitting across from Juby at the end window. With that profile it had to be him. And now that he stood before her in the full light of day she saw how like the old man he was. Deadringer, in fact, just younger. Much younger. He even had his nose, in embryo.

'Er...'

It was meant as a tug to Juby, who'd continued walking a little way and now stood, like the boy, gazing out to sea. He didn't seem to have heard her, but the boy must have, for he looked at her in surprise, as though only now aware of her. Then he opened his mouth to speak.

And faded out of existence.

12

It wasn't until the boy vanished that Midge realized that he'd not seemed to be wholly there anyway. She hadn't been able to see through him exactly, but there'd certainly been something rather less than substantial about him. A ghost? In broad daylight? Whatever the light, she didn't believe in ghosts, ghosts were total hogwash, but hogwash or not, she'd seen something she had no explanation for. Something... ghostlike. Taken aback rather than alarmed by the apparition, she advanced on Juby, intending to tell him what she'd seen, but he began to speak at the sound of her approach.

'Good few ships have gone down around this bay over the years,' he said. 'There was a coastguard station and a signal canon on the Tout till 1910 or thereabouts, but there were still wrecks.'

The moment was past. She shook the almost-there boy away in favor of the immediate, ever-visible world. 'What's the Tout?' she asked, drawing level with her guide.

He gestured to the far left of the bay, a steep promontory. 'Old name for those rocks. Means lookout point. Stand there and look east on a day like today and you can see all the way to St Aldhelm's Head. Look the other way and you'll see Arish Mell, Mupe Bay, and more. Up there's where Davy Miller's house stood,' he added, changing the subject so swiftly that it took a second for her to become aware of it.

'Davy Miller?' she said then. 'That's my dad's name. Only he's usually called Dave.'

'Yes, I was forgetting. You're a Miller. Know much about the Millers of Crowbarrow, do you?'

'I've... never heard of them.'

'What? Someone must've mentioned them, your dad being of their stock and all.'

'Their stock?'

'Didn't his folks come from here?'

'My dad's folks? From here?'

'Thought I heard that someplace,' Juby said.

'Well it's the first I have. These Millers of Crowbarrow...'

'Fishing family. Sort of a clan really, so many of them. As much a part of this stretch as the fossils you can turn up with a spade a little way along. It wouldn't have ever crossed their minds that they'd be forced out of here, but then, in a matter of weeks, they weren't even neighbors any more, and the coast they'd lived by for generations was barred to them.'

'And they were definitely relatives of my dad's?'

'I'm guessing,' Juby said. 'One or two of 'em maybe.'

'Can you tell me anything about them, these Millers?'

'Like what?'

'Well, I don't know. What is there?'

'Well, there was Davy, like I said. His house was tucked away in that nook there. Best views around up there, caught every sunrise and sunset, sheltered from the worst of the gales too.'

'Any others? Other Millers?'

'Oh, stacks. The ones that stood out for me were the brothers, Ethan, Seth and Enoch. Enoch was famous for his fingers. Had five on each hand.'

'Doesn't everyone?'

'Most people have four fingers and a thumb,' Juby said. 'Enoch had a thumb *plus* five fingers. The fifth was a little one tagged on the end, beside the next smallest, which earned him the nickname Sixer. Hell of a fisherman, old Enoch. Then there was Granny Fleur, Londoner originally, mother of Iris and Lily. Iris was married to Ethan... no, I tell a lie, Ethan never married. Iris was Seth's missus. Enoch didn't marry either, but he lived with a woman called Joan, who made fancy hats that she sold at Wareham market.

Another branch of the Millers lived up there, on the – '

He continued in this vein, cataloguing Miller after Miller, where their homes once stood or the sorry remains of them huddled today, the names of husbands, wives, partners, children, and soon Midge was barely listening as she imagined all those hitherto unknown relatives going about their lives here, taking the boats out, hauling the fish in, their kids running along the shore where today only casual visitors and Army personnel came.

'Me and Ed, we often came down here,' Juby said somewhere on the periphery of her thoughts. 'Liked the space, the ocean, the big sky, and if we were early enough, watching the fishermen bang their boots together before climbing into their boats, to get the stones and pebbles out from between the hobnails.'

It's so still here, Midge thought. Still as in dead. There weren't even any of the anticipated gulls. Scared off decades ago, no doubt, by the guns and shellfire that must be deafening when the range was closed to the public.

'Here's another Miller for you,' Juby said. She made herself pay attention. 'When the War Office decided they were taking over the valley, the letter sent to all the householders giving them a month's notice was signed by a Major-General Miller of Southern Command.'

'One of these Millers?' Midge asked.

'If he was, no one claimed him. Coincidence, I expect, but an extra twist of the knife for the Crowbarrow branch.

Most of them, like the Rouklye villagers, felt it their patriotic duty to quit without fuss because they'd been told it was in the nation's interests, but it was too much for some. Old Davy now. They loaded him and Mrs. Davy on a lorry with all their gear and dropped them off at some dump that had been found for them out Stoborough way. Davy took his last breath a week after the move, begging to be brought back. Mind you, he did have the flu, and he was in his ninetie – '

He broke off abruptly, an odd dry rattling sound in his throat, and he sagged, staggered backward groping for something to lean on.

'What is it?' Midge said. 'What's wrong?'

Juby found a fence post and jammed his lower back against it, eyes screwed up tight, the color draining from his face. Midge cast about for help – a summer visitor who just happened to be a doctor or nurse, someone, anyone, who could take charge – but there was only her, and the best she could do was fret and dither helplessly for the two or three minutes it took Juby to open his eyes again. Red-rimmed, watery eyes.

'Okay now?' she asked then.

He cleared his throat. 'Touch of the heat is all.'

His voice was taut, strained, gravely. Tugging his tea-towel of a hanky from his pocket to mop his neck and brow, he failed to notice the small object that flew out with it. Midge stooped, picked it up, turned it over in her hand. It was a carved wooden chess piece, as smooth and shiny as a new conker, jet black, with battlements on top.

'What's that you got there?' Juby asked.

She held the chessman out to him. 'You dropped it.'

He took it from her. 'My talisman. Wouldn't do to lose this, even at this late stage.'

'Talisman?'

'My lucky piece. Always knew I'd come back as long as I had this.' He buffed it up on his sleeve. 'It was Mum's, part of a set she...'

He stopped, and for a moment Midge thought he was going to have another turn. But he'd paused merely to correct himself.

'I mean Aunty Liss. Edwin's mother. I called her Mum too sometimes.' The admission seemed to embarrass him. 'She taught me to play.'

'Play?'

'Chess.'

'Are you any good?'

'Out of practice. No one plays back home.'

He shoved his small piece of the past back in his pocket and broached the tricky little path down to the beach. Midge followed, and was soon crunching over pebbles and coarse sand in his heavy-footed wake.

Given the broadness of the bay, with chalk cliffs rising to one side of it, more modest grassy hills on the other, it was an unassuming beach, and there were very few people on it: a few strollers, three or four families some way along, and in the water just two, a young woman with her small naked child, a pretty little thing with bright blonde curls, lifting her legs high and squealing as the surf hissed about her. The water looked so inviting that Midge slipped off her sandals and ran straight in – and straight out again, screaming silently.

'You get used to it!' the woman with the toddler shouted.

The second time she was more prepared, and soon up to her knees, splashing water on goosefleshed arms, dabbing at her face with her fingertips, shivering exquisitely as icy droplets trickled down her neck.

Juby, too, had entered the water, but no further than the lapping shallows, where foam fizzed between his bare toes, his sandals on the shingle behind him, entwined like exhausted wrestlers. Suddenly he bent double and plunged a hand into the water. Straightening up, he held out his open palm. 'Crowbarrow shells,' he said.

She waded back to look at a small pink and white conch and two brass ammunition cartridges.

'Want them?' he asked.

She would have liked to examine the cartridges at her leisure, maybe take them home as souvenirs, but something made her decline, and then she was glad she had because there was a look in his eye that suggested that her refusal pleased him. He closed his hand, drew it back, and lobbed the three shells as far out to sea as they were willing to go.

It was Juby who decided that they should have an early

lunch. Settling themselves on a broad flat rock toward the back of the beach, they opened Inger's canvas bag and took out the sandwiches, the flask of tea, Midge's preferred bottle of water, and began to eat and sip. With the salt on her lips and binding the ends of her hair, the sun a golden cloth on her skin, all that stopped it being a perfect moment was the absence of gulls and the overabundance of sand flies that had to be constantly batted away. Juby seemed equally content, saying little while he ate, but every so often his eyes would cloud over for reasons Midge could only guess at.

'If you lived round here,' she said, 'in Underthorpe or one of the other villages, you could come here more often. Gran says that apart from August they let people in on a few weekends throughout the year.'

A brusque shake of the head. 'Wouldn't work. Couldn't come and go as I please. No, better to visit once a year like I've been doing. My own terms that way.'

'All right, but why live so far away? Why Sweden?'

'Because that's where I fell off the curb.'

'Uh?'

'Stockholm.'

'Stockholm?'

'I was just passing through, earning a few krona to feed myself, buy a roof over me head for the odd night, and that day, busy street, flutes up me nose, eyes closed, maybe I got carried away by the melody, I don't know, but I lost me balance and next thing I know I'm in the road and traffic's

90

swerving to miss me. One motorbike almost got me, but I was pulled out of the way just in time, and I never wanted to move again. Travel-move, that is.'

'You mean you lost your nerve?'

Juby chuckled dryly. 'Nerve? No. It was who pulled me out of the gutter. Pulled me out, got me to me feet, shoved me pipes back in me pocket, led me away to buy me a beer. And that was it for me. Her too, as it turned out. Still amazes me to this day that she saw something in me.'

'Who was she?'

For a moment it looked as though he didn't know how to say what was on the tip of his tongue, but then he did say something, just one word, but so quietly that Midge couldn't catch it.

'What?' she said. 'Who?'

He looked at her. Seemed to be considering whether to speak up or not, until, again quietly, but audibly: 'Gabriela.'

'Gabriela?'

He looked away again. 'Sweden's where I fell off the curb, Sweden's where I was rescued, Sweden's where my family is.'

'You have family there?'

A tiny nod. 'Married daughter, three grandkids.'

'Grandkids? You have...?'

Him, a grandfather? Hard to imagine, old as he was.

'Two girls,' he said, 'Hanna and Klara, and the boy, Juby, he's the eldest, just turned sixteen. My age when I left here.'

'Juby? Your grandson has the same name as you?'

Another dry chuckle. 'I know, I know, a Swedish boy with an old West Country name. My daughter's idea. Johanna's a very generous person. I've known many generous women in my life, and I'm glad to say my girl's one of 'em.'

'And you speak Swedish, do you?' Midge said.

'I get by. But most Swedes speak English better than I do, so I don't have to bother much of the time.'

'Have you ever brought them here? Your family.'

'Here? To Crowbarrow?'

'And Rouklye.'

He shook his head. 'Only one that ever expressed any interest is the boy. Young Jube can't get enough of it.' He looked at his large brown hands, a half-eaten sandwich dangling from one of them. 'Got a letter from him this morning, matter of fact. Must have written it the day I set out, or the day after. Says he's thinking about me here. Dreaming about being here himself. Isn't that nice?'

'Yes. It is.'

She wondered what might have become of this strange man if he hadn't been forced out of his home all those years ago. With his great beak of a nose, his palest-of-pale gray eyes, the hair just made to be flung around in a gale, he might have forged links with the fishermen of Crowbarrow, joined their ranks even. If the Army hadn't seized the valley and kept it, the cottages around the bay would still be standing, some of them occupied by today's generation of Millers; relatives she might have known and come to visit from time to time. If things had been otherwise she could be sitting here right now watching young cousins running in and out of the water while she listened to the life story of an old Crowbarrow fisherman named Juby Bench.

'What was it like at the end?' she asked quietly.

'The end?'

'Out here, when everyone was leaving.'

'Cold,' he said.

'Cold?'

'Bitter. Coldest December in living memory. The sea was icy.'

'I bet it was.'

'Great sheets of spray striking the cliffs. I came here a lot in the last days, saying my goodbyes...'

He paused. She prompted, with: 'Goodbyes?'

'To the land, the beach... y'know. There was a bad storm one night. I stood up there on the cliff through much of it. The valley was mostly clear by the deadline, just a handful still waiting for transport. Then the lorries took the last of us, and that was it. Should'a known we wouldn't be coming back. Nothing could've felt more like the end.'

As he finished, Midge's gaze drifted up to the cliffs, and she saw, right on the edge, a tall young figure with a wild mop of hair, staring out to sea.

13

They returned to the village by an alternative route, on a narrow footpath along the top of the numbered hill they'd paralleled on the trek to Crowbarrow. This was the clifftop hike Juby had mentioned enjoying as a lad. Even for the lad he once was it must have been a bit of a slog, and it was soon obvious that in his early seventies he was far from fit enough to undertake the walk with ease. On the way up the first of what turned out to be just one of many precipitous stretches, Midge asked him what he did in Sweden.

'What do you mean what did I do?' he said, already breathing hard.

'For a living.'

'Well, these days I live off my pension and the few pennies I've saved, but I've been a factory hand, window-cleaner, road sweeper, painter and decorator, I worked on the odd building site and... a few other things. Nothing very impressive.'

'Always in Sweden?'

'No, all over, even after I was supposed to have settled down. In Belgium one time I was a clown.'

'A clown?'

'In a circus.'

She laughed. '*You* were a circus *clown*?'

'Only for a month. They sacked me. Said I scared the kids. I used to run across the ring and scream in their faces. I thought it was funny. Some adults didn't. One job I had was as a waiter in an restaurant in Frankfurt. English restaurant. Made out I was German for the tourists. Put on a heavy accent and had a real gift for looking down my nose at them from a great height.'

After this he lapsed into a rasping silence, needing what breath he could grab for the ever-upward trudge. To their right as they climbed, in the grass between the path and the ocean, they passed notice after notice warning them that the cliff was 'unstable'. To their left, behind strings of barbed-wire, metal signs were set in the ground.

DANGER

UNEXPLODED

SHELLS

KEEP OUT

'Are you sure we're allowed up here?' Midge asked.

'Course. If we weren't, what'd be the point of the signs?'

'And this is definitely the way back?'

'The path should swing down toward the car park some way along. Always used to anyway. But if they've stuck a barrier somewhere ahead we can always jog down the hill and across the fields.'

'Oh, great. Through the unexploded shells.'

'You worry too much,' Juby said, and puffed on.

After twenty minutes of this, Midge's clothes were sticking to her and Juby's shirt clung to him like a second skin. He was very red in the face now, and each breath was drawn as a wheeze, expelled as a gasp, but when she asked him if he wanted to stop for a rest he waved an impatient hand and toiled on, mopping his brow and neck with his enormous hanky. Next time, she made out that it was she who needed the break.

'It's so hot! Can't we sit down for a minute?'

This he could accept – 'Sure, no rush' – it being for her benefit rather than his.

Arduous as the climb was under the relentless sun, the views were an unexpected compensation for Midge, who as a rule had little time for scenery. To one side, the many luminous blue glimpses of the ocean formed an eventual horizon that stretched for miles; on the other, beyond the fenced-off woods and scattered remnants of Rouklye village, green and russet hills hemmed the valley. Below them, positioned like a warning or threat on a man-made plateau, sat the three long-barrelled tanks and the numbered boards they'd seen from below.

After a few minutes' rest Juby was on his feet again, storming ahead along the track, and she was following, but before long his predicted downward route materialized. The path, bordered by yellow markers and notices reminding walkers that it was dangerous to leave it, wended through frayed meadows accessed by weathered stiles and squealing iron gates. For Midge it was a pleasure to descend, but Juby's breath still rasped badly and by the time they reached the cattle grid they'd gazed over before taking the track to Crowbarrow, he looked as if another yard would finish him.

They were almost at the little bridge that led to the car park when Juby said: 'I need to pee.'

'Is there anywhere here *to* pee?' Midge asked.

'There's anywhere you want, long as no wardens catch you.'

'Someplace civilized would be nice. Like a building?'

'Civilized, judge for yourself, but there's a building. Of sorts.'

'Of sorts' seemed a fair description for the stinking hut that he led her to, just round the corner from the bridge, sensibly concealed by bushes. It had two entrances and two divided inner sections, one with a urine-soaked floor for men to stand on, the other with badly-scuffed plastic seats (black) that you wouldn't want to introduce your rear end to. Midge, nose wrinkled as tightly as it would go, eyes half shut to avoid taking in more of her surroundings than she had to, just about managed without sitting.

Rejoining Juby outside, she found his breathing less ragged and that he seemed lighter of heart than before. When she asked if the toilet was a relic from the old days, his croaky reply sounded very nearly like laughter.

'No. No. That's a modern construction.'

As they were crossing the car park, however, he became more subdued, as though something unpleasant had occurred to him, and when he deposited the depleted refreshment bag in the overheated car but showed no inclination to head back to Underthorpe, she suggested that he go off on his own for a while, and without further discussion he set about doing so while she settled herself on the curved stone seat set into the wall at the church end of Post Office Row.

There were trees here – their shade was more than merely welcome – and as she lolled, eyes closed, bare legs stretched out before her, she felt more content than she had for some time, without quite knowing why. Every now and then footsteps and voices came and went. She paid no attention to what was said, but, peeking occasionally through her lashes, glimpsed couples or parents with children, and once or twice no one at all. The absence of physical forms to accompany some of the voices did not disturb her unduly. She didn't feel threatened by them, any more than she'd felt threatened by the disappearing boy earlier. They were part of the place, along with the ruins, nothing more.

'Popping down to the house, wanta come?'

She squinted up at the long streak of darkness with its unruly head in the sun. She would rather have stayed where she was but he'd invited her to accompany him, which must mean that he wasn't yet sick of...

'Okay. Sure.'

She got up and trailed after him, past the schoolhouse and down the narrow sloping path to his childhood home within its shroud of wire and weeds and warnings.

'See that window?' he said as she joined him, still unaware that while he could see a fair portion of the house she had to stand on tiptoe just to glimpse the top third.

'Which one?'

'The upstairs one, in the middle.'

She could see a bit of it, only a bit.

'Some mornings back home,' he said, 'I wake up and I'm in that room, eleven, twelve, thirteen years old. My eyes are still shut, but I know it's just getting light, and I lie there waiting for the first bird to start up. Then it comes, this solo sound, and then there's a warble from another quarter, and a whistle, a shriek, a flap of feathers, till there's a hundred of 'em, might be a thousand, and the woods are bursting with their unholy racket, and it's like... it's as though...'

She waited, but for Juby words had ceased to be necessary. He was back in his childhood, head tilted as he listened to his long dead birds.

Midge listened too. Heard nothing.

14

In theory, meals at her grandparents' were never at a set

time. This, according to Inger, was because their lives weren't sliced up into neat bite-sized portions to fit round television schedules. There was no television in the house: Inger's decree. Edwin had an alternative view on the timing of meals but kept it to himself, aiming, during weekdays at least, to put food on the table for six in order to be down the garden in his Pottering Shed by seven to make the most of his secret life.

Six o'clock was long gone this evening, however, and as yet there'd been no call to go and eat, but this was fine by Midge, up in her room writing to Nessa. Nessa who, with her enviably good looks and effortless charm, could express herself concisely and tellingly and was good at everything she wanted to be good at, on top of which the boys only had eyes for her when the two of them were out together. She sometimes wondered why Ness bothered with her. Probably for no other reason than that they'd been neighbors, houses right next door to one another on the newish estate, for the entire eight years since Midge's parents had decided to move there rather than stay in Michigan, where her friends since birth lived. Another year and Ness was bound to move on, find friends more like herself − attractive, quick-witted, mistresses of any situation − while she, frowzy, colorless Midge, would continue to be condemned to grim little cells like this while her parents swanned about the world on various noble or foolish missions.

But such comparisons were far from uppermost in her

mind this early evening as she sat writing at the little table by the window, pausing every now and then to decide how best to express this or that sensation, describe that or this observation or scene. There was quite a lot about Juby, as entertainment for a friend. She wrote about their breakfast at The Ferryman, the long walk to the coast, the sweaty hike back along the high cliff. She also described the broad, undistinguished bay overlooked by the wretched remains of cottages that might once have housed relatives of hers. And this time she mentioned the almost-there boy, on the track to Crowbarrow. When talking about the boy, she adopted a mildly self-mocking tone so that her friend, if she didn't believe her, wouldn't think she'd lost it. It was the longest letter she'd ever written to anyone, but as she wrote she realized that although she missed the company of people her own age it was starting to get just a little bit more interesting here.

When she'd filed the finished letter with the one she'd written a few days ago, to post around the time Ness got back from her vacation, she again inspected her private picture gallery. Even more of the old photos meant something now. She couldn't place every building, but some of the ones that Juby had pointed out were there, and where several of the names underneath still meant nothing to her, she thought she recognized that hill, that path, that bit of wall, and this pleased her.

When she was eventually called down to eat, by Inger,

she found just two places at the table, each with a bowl containing a portion of some sort of pasta, prepared by Inger herself.

'Where's Grandpa?'

'He's not talking to me,' Inger said.

'Why, what have you done?'

'I allowed you to go to Rouklye with Juby again.'

Midge sat down and eyed, with little enthusiasm, the food in front of her. If Edwin had prepared the meal it would probably have been something quite good, and he'd try to make her smile while they were eating, but instead there was this, and he'd gone off in a temper, leaving a cheerless atmosphere behind him. She tendered a sample of the pasta to her mouth, waited a second or two for her taste buds to leap into action, and decided that it could be worse.

'Gran...'

'Midge, darling, you don't think, do you, that you could experiment with calling me something else? I mean "Gran" has never seemed quite *me* somehow.'

'I wouldn't know what else to call you.'

'Try Inger.'

'Oh, I couldn't.' (Not to your face anyway, she thought.)

'Ah well. What was it you wanted to say?'

'You know that chess set in my room?'

'Chess set... chess set...' Inger mused; then: 'Oh, yes, that old thing. Belonged to Lisette.'

'Lisette?'

'Edwin's mum.'

'I never knew her,' Midge said.

'No, she died before you were born. I only met her twice myself. Sparky old dame. You don't play, do you? It's years since I played, and Edwin has no interest.'

She shook her head. 'There's a piece missing anyway. That's what I wanted to ask about.'

'Mm. One of the rooks. Even Edwin doesn't know what happened to that.'

'No, the missing piece isn't a bird,' Midge said. 'It's a castle.'

'The pieces with battlements are usually called rooks,' Inger informed her.

'Rooks? Are you sure?'

Inger was. Popping a distracted forkful of pasta into her mouth, Midge recalled what Juby had told her on the bridge over the stream before they set off for Crowbarrow. How as a boy in Rouklye he loved the sound of the rooks, and that there hadn't been any in the valley since the people were evicted. *I always had this idea that if the rooks came back, if just one returned...* Even at the time she'd been fairly sure what was in his mind: *...if just one returned everything would be all right again.* Was that what he was doing when he came back each year with the chess piece in his pocket, bringing a 'rook' back where it belonged, as if such a gesture would restore everything? It was on the tip of her tongue to say where the missing piece was, but she bit it back, along with the mouthful of pasta, on the grounds that it wasn't her place to do so.

Instead she said: 'Juby. He looks a bit like a rook, don't you think?'

'Juby looks like a chessman?' Inger said.

'No, the bird. That suit of his, the way he stalks about, even his nose – sort of... beaklike.'

Inger laughed. 'Now that you mention it, I think I thought something of the sort myself when I first saw him.'

'In Amsterdam,' Midge said.

'He told you about Amsterdam?'

'Mentioned it.'

'Yes, well there he was with those flute things up that great hooter of his, making a dreadful noise – he was no musician, that young man – but the look of him! Quite the tallest fellow I'd ever seen, and with so much hair, dark in those days. He wore this long black cape, fastened at the neck with a silver chain – said he'd "borrowed" it from a copper – and he stood on one leg while he played, the other folded up under him somehow. I don't know if rooks stand on one leg, but yes, all in all, very rook-like.'

'He told me he'd been out of England for years, but didn't say why,' Midge said.

Inger traced patterns in her pasta with her fork. She seemed to have lost interest in it as food.

'I suppose you could say that he fled.'

'Fled?'

'To avoid conscription.'

'Conscription?'

'In this country, for quite a long time after the war, every able-bodied young man was obliged to spend a couple of years in the armed forces. Juby's call-up papers must have come a year or two after the military took over his precious valley, and nothing would have induced him to join the ranks of the people who'd kicked him out – so he skedaddled to the Continent and didn't come back till the mid-fifties.'

'When you came with him?'

Inger dropped her fork and pushed her plate away. 'For the walk and for my sins, having no idea I would grow old and senile here. Who knows where I'd be today, what I'd be doing, if he hadn't abandoned me during our day-trip to Rouklye?'

'Day-trip? Abandoned you?'

'Skipped that bit, did he?' Inger said with a half-smile. 'The first thing he wanted to do when we got to Dorset was check out his old stamping ground. He hooked up with Edwin for the first time in years and we both accompanied him. The valley wasn't open to the public then, so we had to go in by a covert way they used as boys. Edwin hadn't been back since the evacuation, but living locally he had some notion of what to expect. Poor Juby, though, he wasn't prepared at all.'

'For the ruins?'

'They weren't quite ruins then, though from the look of

things the buildings had been used for heavy target practice. The US Army had control of the village in the early days and by all accounts they treated it with respect, but then the British paras took over, and...'

She paused. 'Yes?' Midge said.

'They showed rather less respect for the place. Chimneys were toppled, roofs allowed to cave in – or deliberately demolished, I don't know – Army vehicles were rammed into walls and left to rust, there was litter everywhere, oil drums, bottles, graffiti, excrement and used condoms in former living rooms. Juby was horrified. All those years he'd been imagining Rouklye as he'd last seen it, and there it was, so bleak, so filthy, abused. He turned on his heel and left without a word, to me or anyone else.'

'But you stayed?'

'I... yes. Stayed.'

'Why?'

'Because...' Inger sought reasons, clutched at straws. 'Because it suited me, I think. Because I didn't fancy going all the way back to Norway by myself, because Edwin was rather taken with me...'

'Taken with you?'

'He made me laugh. I always had a soft spot for men who make me laugh.'

Midge almost remarked that he didn't seem to make her laugh much these days, but resisted.

'When did you see him next – Juby?'

Inger sat back in her chair and gazed at her across the table. 'You're very curious all of a sudden. A day or two ago you didn't seem bothered about anything, and now you're into life histories. What brings this on?'

'Does there have to be a reason?' Midge said, only just managing not to visibly wilt before her grandmother's bland scrutiny.

'No. Not really. The next time we heard from Juby was the early nineteen-sixties. A letter from Sweden in which he said his wife had passed away. We had no idea he was married till then. He sent a photo. Nice-looking girl. Very lively face. Gabriela. Died from a brain hemorrhage, quite unexpectedly, no warning. She collapsed one afternoon in the garden, Juby called an ambulance, but she was dead on arrival at the hospital.'

'That's terrible,' Midge said.

'It is. I can't imagine how it must have affected him. He was always more sensitive than he liked to let on. Still is, I believe.'

'But after her... his wife... he stayed in Sweden?'

'They had a young daughter at school in Uppsala. But he started to come over occasionally after Gabriela's death. He would always go to Rouklye, sneak in past the guards. It wasn't until the seventies, when pressure groups finally persuaded the MoD to let the public in every so often, that they began tidying the village up, removing dilapidated or dangerous roofs, unsafe ceilings, stairs, all the mess they'd made. Since then Juby's visited every August bar four, when he was unwell or needed at home.'

'Have you met his daughter? His grandchildren?'

'No. Far as I know the Müellers have never set foot in England, and Edwin's not a great traveler, so...'

Midge's eyes popped. 'Did you say Müeller?'

'His daughter's husband is German, which means it's the children's surname too.'

'But Müeller,' Midge said. 'Müeller, of all names.'

That night, she dreamed of Rouklye again. Rouklye with all the roofs, windows and doors in place, though again without people. But then, in the dream, the almost-there boy emerged from the post office, looked first one way, then the other, and finally became aware of her. He smiled when he saw her; started toward her, and was almost within reach when she woke with a start, and the boy, and habitable Rouklye, tumbled back into the night.

15

This morning, another quiet one, Inger sat in her little office, feet on desk, indulging in one of the four Balkan Sobranies she allowed herself each day, while Midge, for something to do following the departure of the last empty-handed browser, tidied tightly-packed shelves that didn't really need tidying. The second-hand section demanded a little more attention, however, and she was giving it that little bit when her eye was caught by a name on the spine of a slim green hardback entitled *On the Bleak Ridge*. The name – of the author – was William Rainey. Plucking the book from the shelf, she found it to be a collection of poems. She took it to the office and held it up for Inger's inspection.

'Is this someone I should know about?' she asked.

'Where'd you find that?' Inger said.

'Second-hand section.'

'It was probably part of a job lot. People come in sometimes with bags or boxes of books they have no use for and I give them a few charitable pennies and they – the books – sit for years on the shelf, never looked at or bought by a living soul. Waste of space really, and my pennies.'

'But who is he? Is or was? A relative of Grandpa's?'

'Not one that he's mentioned, far as I recall.'

She held her hand out and Midge placed the book in it. Inger opened it at the copyright page.

'Tulkinghorn Press, Maycomb, AL, 1987,' she read. 'American publication then, which suggests that the author's American too, rather than a local relative of Edwin's. No idea how it ended up here, who brought it to me, or...' She turned a few pages, paused at one, smiled at a line she read there, and went on, in a vague, distracted sort of way. 'You know, if

I were a writer... a novelist... I could tell quite a tale of the stories behind some of the books that fall into the hands of a second-hand dealer. Every second-hand book has a history all of its own. Someone brings a book to me, say, having no use for it, or maybe it was a gift they never cared for, or it belonged to a recently-deceased parent. If the parent, why did she or he own it? Was it a gift or a private purchase? Was it read and enjoyed, was it started but not finished, and if it wasn't finished why wasn't it? Because it didn't sufficiently capture the reader's imagination or because of some personal disruption: divorce, death, a move to another house? Yes, every used book carries an exclusive unrecorded backstory, as lost to the rest of us in our own little worlds as it might have been to the individual who brought it in. Quite interesting, that, when you think about it, eh?' She glanced at Midge, who was gazing vacantly along the street. 'Or not,' she concluded, closing the book and proffering it. 'Keep it if you want.'

Midge had little interest in a book of poems but took it anyway, just as the bell on the shop door jangled and a voice called out.

'Hello! Anyone alive in here?'

Inger sighed – 'Oh, God, and it was such a peaceful morning' – stubbed out her cigarette, and left the office, followed hesitantly by Midge.

'Hi, Midge,' Jilly Barstow said. 'Busy helping Granny?'

'Granny!' Inger bellowed. 'Gran's bad enough, but

Granny? Out of my shop, woman, out, out!'

Jilly came further in.

'I imagine you've come for your book,' Inger said. Jilly went blank. 'The cookery tome by that grinning TV chef idiot that you ordered last week...?'

'It's in already?'

'We're nothing if not efficient here.' Inger ducked below the counter for the book and held it up for Jilly's inspection. 'Do the honors, will you, Midge?' She handed her the book. 'She wraps better than I do,' she told Jilly.

Jilly touched her hair with her fingertips in case a whisper of breeze had wheedled its way through the wall of heat outside and dared disturb a strand. 'I really came in for something else,' she said. 'Some-*one* else.'

'Oh?'

Pouncing on a neat pile of local event info leaflets with the sole intention, it seemed, of making a mess of them, Jilly elaborated. 'I was wondering if Midge would care to join us for lunch and spend some more time with Nat. And Henrietta, of course, though Henry's quite self-sufficient and independent for her age. She can always find ways to amuse herself.'

Midge had given her grandmother a fairly precise account of her encounter with Nathaniel and received a pledge that she would not have to endure his company again. But here she was being asked to offer her up for further sacrifice. Could she refuse? Midge attempted telepathy: *Save me. Please. I'll do anything, just don't let her take me.*

'Driving you up the wall, is he?' Inger said to Jilly.

The leaflets dropped from Jilly's fingers. Her eyes were large and helpless. 'All the way to the bloomin' ceiling.'

A lesser woman might have weakened at this and handed her granddaughter over screaming, but Inger was made of sterner stuff.

'You have my sympathies, dear, but I'm afraid Midge has a prior engagement.' She swung a reassuring arm round her assistant's shoulders. 'We have to visit her incontinent Uncle Jim in a nursing home in Weymouth.'

'You've never mentioned an Uncle Jim in a nursing home,' Jilly said suspiciously.

Inger shook her head sadly. 'We don't talk about him.'

'Oh. Well perhaps they'll get together at the barbecue.'

Inger's fingers crushed Midge's shoulder. 'Barbecue?'

'You haven't forgotten my High Summer Barbie on Saturday?'

'Forgotten?' Inger said, rather too hastily. 'Of course we haven't forgotten. We were just saying how much we're looking forward to it. Weren't we, Midge?'

She dug her fingernails into the already damaged shoulder and shot its owner a lightning glance of dismay to show her true feelings about the barbecue. Midge made a high-pitched 'Mm!' sound. Those nails were sharp.

When Jilly had gone Midge said: 'Uncle Jim in a nursing home?'

Inger grinned. 'Spur of the moment relative.'

'But what if she comes back and we're still here?'

The grin dissolved. 'P'rhaps we'd better go out anyway.'

'What, shut the shop?'

'Oh, I couldn't do that, this is my busiest month.'

'Not so busy today,' Midge pointed out.

'It'll pick up this afternoon. Have to call in the reserves again. Once I track him down. I don't know where that man gets to half the time.'

16

'Where are we going?' she asked as they climbed into the Volvo after lunch.

'I told Jilly Weymouth, so why not Weymouth?' Inger said, adjusting her sunglasses. 'Think we'll give the nursing home a miss though, don't you, seeing as we're a bit short of incontinent Uncle Jims?'

She started the car, looked left and right, ignored the evidence of her own eyes, and flung it across the road so that the red sports car doing forty down the high street was forced to brake hard. The driver blasted her with his horn.

'Road hog!' Inger yelled into the rear-view mirror.

With a business to run, Inger left Underthorpe far less often than she might have wished, so Weymouth made a change for her too. 'We should take you out more often,' she said as they strolled through the town after parking the car. 'It's not fair on you, cooped up inside all day, specially in weather like this. Pity about all these people, though. People should be banned, along with traffic.'

That leisurely afternoon would turn out to be the longest period of time that Midge had ever spent alone in her grandmother's company outside the shop, and it wasn't such bad company at that, she found. In her late-sixties, tall, slim, straight-backed, alert, Inger wasn't much less vivacious than she'd been in her twenties, or much less shapely. Men of all ages eyed her up in passing, and she reveled in it, quite blatantly, to Midge's occasional embarrassment and secret pride. A gran who turned men's heads: now wasn't *that* something? She must have driven them wild when she first walked into Dorset with Juby all those years ago. No wonder Edwin had been drawn to her. This afternoon she wore Roman-style sandals, a white cotton skirt (which became translucent when the sun was behind or in front of her), and a shirt of turquoise silk. No bra. Very *evidently* no bra. She'd drawn her hair back, fitted earrings that swung like golden nooses, and wore more bangles on her wrists than Midge even possessed. If I look half that sexy at a third of her age, she thought, I won't complain.

Inger would also have worn the hat she kept in the car had she not, just as they were setting out, slammed the boot on it and effectively sliced it in two. In need of a replacement she insisted on Midge having one as well, so they went into a seafront gift shop where Midge chose a broad-brimmed straw effort with ragged edges and Inger opted for a white mini sombrero with KISS ME SLOW on the front. When she saw herself in the mirror she laughed like a Norwegian drain. Midge covered her eyes.

It came as no surprise that Inger was a mine of information about Weymouth. She was a mine of information about many things, ascribing her wide-ranging knowledge of trivia to 'all those years sitting on my duff in the shop, reading anything that comes to hand while waiting for waste-of-space browsers.' Weymouth, as a subject, would not ordinarily have piqued Midge's interest in the slightest, but presented by Inger, with her lively delivery and her slight but unusual accent, even the dullest of facts sounded as if they stood a chance of being worth listening to any time now. Her history teacher would have had her stifling a yawn with: 'Henry VIII turned Weymouth harbor into a naval base'. Coming from Inger she found herself paying attention and thinking that she would remember that.

One of her fragments of enlightenment caused quite a laugh, if only for Midge. They were strolling along the Esplanade, having just bought cones of Mr. Mario ice-cream from a van adorned with painted balloons, and Inger was telling Midge, who hadn't asked, how George III, sampling the waters here in the late seventeen hundreds, had become the first recorded English monarch to take a voluntary dip in the sea. 'A vastly stupid act that started the craze for sea bathing that's with us still,' she said. 'When you think that Georgie boy was completely off his twig, one can but wonder about the sanity of the scores of lemmings who follow his example every summer. I mean to say, just *look* at them all!'

At 'just *look* at them all' the hand holding the Mr. Mario flew out to indicate the beach packed with sunbathers, swimmers and paddlers. The cone remained in her grip, but the soft vanilla ice, expelled by the jerk of her arm, leapt in a high arc and came down on a shoulder of a deckchair attendant chatting with a group of seniors. The attendant looked from his book of tickets to the large white spreading epaulet just below his right ear. His mouth dropped open – not to sample a free Mr. Mario – and his amazed eyes lifted to an enormous seagull gliding innocently overhead.

They were sitting on a bench facing the sea when Midge asked Inger what she knew of Rouklye.

'Well, I know as much as anyone who's lived in the vicinity for as long as I have,' she replied. 'Which let me tell you is *far* too long. What do you want to know?'

She wasn't sure; admitted this.

'Well, going right back, there was a Roman settlement in the valley. Evidence of Iron Age activity's been found there too, apparently, and – '

'I'm thinking a bit more recently,' Midge said.

Inger stopped. 'I'm sure you are. But nothing that exists today would even *be* there if not for its history.'

'Yes, of course, but – '

'Rouklye village was a self-contained community for hundreds of years, during which time it underwent many changes of ownership before falling into the hands of a single family for almost three centuries. Then, during the first third of *this* century, much of the surrounding area was acquired by the War Office for training purposes, and when the 1939 war came they saw their chance to get their mitts on the rest – and took it, in the most literal sense, chucking all the residents out. You've seen the end result of *that*,' she added.

'Yes...'

'I'd only been there once myself before the day you and I went there with Juby,' Inger said.

'When was that?'

'Oh, way back. Before you were born. It was just me and Kris and Dave, they hadn't been together very long, I don't recall where Edwin was, skiving off somewhere, no doubt.'

'What did you do there?'

'Do there? In Rouklye? Same as everyone else, nosed around, moaned about the heat, it was a day like today, too warm for comfort. Dave and I spent most of the time in the church, it was cooler in there, while Kris wandered about elsewhere. She's always loved warmth and sunshine, that girl, doesn't get it from me.'

'My dad never goes in churches,' Midge said.

'Well, he did that time. His idea, in fact. He wanted to check out some family history.'

'Family history?'

'There are display boards in there with dates, photos, names of former villagers, the families out Crowbarrow way. It was the Crowbarrow folk that he was particularly interested in. Millers.'

'I've seen some ruined properties where people named Miller once lived,' Midge said.

'Dave was looking for snaps of his dad as a boy. Dad and grandparents. They were among those heaved out in forty-three, and possibly the only ones to go to America from there. No idea how they managed that. From what I've read, no Rouklye resident had any money other than the gentry at the Big House, and the blessed Rector.'

'And there are pictures of them in the church? Dad's father, grandparents?'

'Don't ask me,' Inger said.

'But you were there with him.'

'I had other interests, like fanning myself cool in a pew. I do remember that by the time we left he was looking pretty glum, though.'

'Glum?'

'Downcast. My guess is that he either found what he was looking for or was saddened by the sight of them as young people in old photos.'

'If his father-to-be hadn't gone to America...'

'He wouldn't have met your grandmother,' said Inger.

'No. He wouldn't.'

'And they wouldn't have had your dad, and he, in turn, wouldn't have met my daughter, who just happened to be in New York at the time, working in the perfume section of some big department store... Lacey's... Casey's...'

'Macy's,' Midge said.

'Kris hated that job. Said it swore her off perfume for life. But it was there that he saw her and took a shine to her and where she failed to resist his smarm, and... well, here *you* are.'

'Here *I* am,' Midge said. 'With you, today.'

Inger flashed her one of her big broad grins. 'A detail for which you might be surprised to hear, my darling, that I'm rather grateful.'

Silence fell for a short while until Inger indicated an amusement arcade across the road.

'What say we go over there and squander some loot on pointless games and rigged slot machines?'

'I don't have any loot,' Midge said.

From thin air Inger produced a twenty pound note, which she stuffed into Midge's hand – 'What're you talking about, course you do!' – flipped her hat to a rakish angle, and marched to the curb, from where she stood glaring at the holiday traffic that streamed between her and the arcade. Midge joined her a second after she walked into the road, hand held high to inform the traffic rushing toward her at breakneck speed that it had better watch itself or it would answer to her. Brakes squealed. Mouths twisted in anger.

Inger Bjølstad was in town.

17

While Edwin cooked the meal that night and was at the table to eat with them, he kept his eyes on his plate throughout, said little, and gruffly excused himself the moment he was done instead of waiting for the others to finish and clearing away as he usually did. When he left the room Inger rolled her eyes in irritation.

'The man's a *child*.'

After they'd washed up – something else Edwin usually did – Inger, determined to 'put an end to this nonsense', sent Midge down the garden on a particular errand. Never having seen her grandfather in a really bad mood before, she approached his shed rather timidly. The notice on the closed door did nothing to embolden her.

PRIVATE!
NO HAWKERS
NO JEHOVAH'S WITNESSES
NO NORWEGIANS

The Pottering Shed was Edwin Rainey's bolt-hole. The place he went to when he wanted to be in his own world rather than someone else's. The shed had been delivered in kit form five years ago and had remained unconstructed for some eighteen months while he puzzled over the assembly instructions in Italian, German, French and broken English, and stared at all the little polythene bags of screws, washers and other things that didn't generally play a very important role in his life. Occasionally during this time he hoisted a panel of wood to try and imagine how the shed would look when built, but that was as far as he got until Fred Gittens, a neighbor whose wife had recently left him (also leaving him with time on his hands), joined him in the instruction-solving. Between them they decided what should go where, and erected the shed. The day they finished this monumental task they went over to the Ferryman to celebrate. By the time they returned from the celebratory drink the shed had collapsed, so they went back to the Ferryman to drown their sorrows. The shed might have remained in this forlorn state until it rotted if not for Fred's younger brother Tom. Tom Gittens, builder by trade, didn't need instructions in any language. He assembled the shed almost single-handedly in one hour thirty-five minutes. This time it did not fall down.

One of the things Edwin did to occupy himself in his shed was work on construction kits. In the early days these kits had provided more frustration than satisfaction, as few of the models he'd attempted had ended up bearing more than a passing resemblance to the pictures on the boxes. But then, a while ago, he'd come up with a brilliant solution: only buy kits marked 'For 10 and Under'. As a result the Pottering Shed was now home to a cornucopia of realistic miniature planes, spaceships, boats, automobiles and castles. Some of them were even painted, but he'd given this up when he discovered that painting was another skill he had yet to acquire.

The Pottering Shed was also where Edwin kept the four stamp albums of his youth and his little portable television. He'd told no one about the TV because he didn't want it getting back to Inger, whose dislike of the medium was so extreme that even in his garden sanctuary he kept the sound well down for fear her Nordic antennae would pick it up from the house. To cut the risk of her barging in and spotting the TV, he kept the door locked at all times, when he was in the shed as well as when he was not. What he didn't know was that one evening a few weeks ago, anxious to get to The Ferryman for a swift half before closing, he'd bungled the locking process and the door had swung open a couple of inches as he scuttled past Inger on her way to fetch the washing from the line. Inger had never found the shed open before, and, being a naturally curious person, had not gone out of her way to resist the urge to look inside. She had not mentioned what she saw there, to Edwin or anyone else. For now, the knowing was sufficient.

When he heard a nervous little tap on the door Edwin tumbled out of the lumpy old armchair he'd bought for a tenner at an auction in Church Knowle, threw himself headlong at the TV, and flicked off the sentimental American sitcom he'd not been laughing at.

'Who is it?'

'It's me.'

'Who's me?'

'Midge.'

He covered the set with a blanket kept handy for such thoughtless interruptions (which rarely occurred), unlocked the door, and peered out with one eye to check that it was indeed Midge and not some impersonator trying to fool him.

'Gran thought you might like a cup of tea.'

He eyed the white cup and saucer in her hand. 'Your gran's never brought me a cup of tea out here. Or had one sent to me. Never ever. And I have my own kettle, she knows that.'

'I'll take it back if you like,' Midge said, hoping he would agree so she could make a swift return to the house. As it was she who'd gone to Rouklye with Juby, she assumed that his anger must, in part, be aimed at her, which made her uncomfortable in his presence.

'No, it's all right. Might as well have it as you've taken the trouble.'

He opened the door a bit more and extended his hand for the cup and saucer.

'She sent this too.' Midge held out an envelope.

'What is it, the bill?'

'She didn't say.' He took the envelope in his other hand,

even more suspicious of it than the tea, turned it over, sniffed it, held it up to the light. 'She said to tell you to read it while I'm here.'

'She wants a written reply?'

'I don't know.'

'Hm! Well – you better come in.'

Having no idea what an honor was being bestowed upon her, she entered.

The shed – a comfortable mess, just the way Edwin liked it – smelt of wood and glue and enclosed man. The white roller blinds pulled down over the windows were designed to let in the light but not be seen through. It was very warm in there in spite of the small electric fan. The fan was set on 'rotate', which meant that it swept the interior, left to right, right to left, fanning each part in turn. Every time it came back to the middle, where the door was, Midge's hair stood on end. Edwin, with his wispy little side bits, had no such problem.

''Scuse the mess.'

'This is nothing, you should see my room at home.' Her room at home wasn't anything like as bad as this, but it seemed the thing to say.

'Park your hind-quarters.'

She looked for somewhere to sit. The choice was either the lumpy old armchair or the high stool at the workbench. She opted for the stool and surveyed the bench, which hosted an electric kettle, several mugs well overdue for a wash, a chipped plate of long-retired sandwich crusts, a motley assortment of unpainted models, and the secret TV under the blanket.

Edwin set down the cup and saucer and opened the envelope. Reading Inger's note, he was frowning in seconds.

'Is there an answer?' Midge asked.

'Oh, there's an answer all right. But I think I'll deliver it personally. Stay here!'

Yanking the door back, he charged out, leaving it swinging. Midge slipped off the stool and, through the vertical slit between the door's hinges, watched him stalk up the path. Inger had positioned herself at the kitchen window in anticipation of just such a response, and as he approached she leaned forward, daring him to confront her. Edwin's step faltered. He knew that look. It said 'Mess with me, Rainey, and you're a carcass.' For almost half a minute the two stood glaring at one another through the glass, then Edwin squared his shoulders, held the note up, and ripped it into small pieces, which he flicked defiantly into the air. Finally, he whirled about and stormed back up the path.

Midge rushed to the stool. Her hand shook a little as she reached for something to pretend to be examining, and picked up a small model helicopter. One of the rotor blades immediately fell off. She put the model down at once and pushed it away from her in a 'nothing to do with me,' sort of way.

If she'd glanced toward the door upon Edwin's return

she would have seen his entire demeanor change radically as he entered and the bright light of rebellion fade from his eye. His hands fell limply to his sides as he walked to his chair, for once living, rather than playing, the part of Poor Little Downtrodden Man. She heard the creak of the armchair as he sat, and waited, fingers tightly laced to prevent their reaching out and destroying anything else.

'I've been ordered by she-who-must-be-obeyed,' Edwin said quietly to her back, 'to tell you why I get so vexed about Juby and Rouklye.'

It was something that had worked its way under his skin over the years and scratched and scratched and scratched away until it was a full-blown weeping sore. Personal as it was, he might not have shared it with Midge at any point if Inger's note hadn't informed him that if he didn't clear the air this very evening ('so the girl can stop thinking it's her fault') he could kiss goodbye to a quiet life. It wasn't easy finding the words, though, and all Midge could hear while he struggled to locate a few was such a silence that she began to wonder if he was all right. In the end she turned to see. No, he hadn't quietly died, he was just sitting there, deep in his chair, looking very small and ineffectual. The look of him, from her elevated position on the high stool, fortified her nerve.

'Juby and Rouklye?'

It must have been the nudge he needed, because he scowled anew and jerked forward in his chair, shoulders hunched.

'Juby and Rouklye!' It was so very nearly a roar that it took all of her nerve not to run to the door. 'I'll tell you about Juby and Rouklye!' he said, just a bit less vehemently. 'Every August, rain, hail or shine, that man tootles over from Sweden in his old banger to tell anyone who'll lend him an ear what life used to be like in his perfect English village. Then, having filled a whole new batch of gullible heads with his sentimental twaddle, he shoves off home again, mission accomplished. It makes me mad at the best of times, but now he's filling *your* head with it, and it boils my *blood*!'

Midge stared. Could it really be that two men in their seventies who were boys together in the same village had fallen out because they disagreed about what it was like living there? How idiotic. How ludicrous. How unbelievably pathetic.

Edwin caught her incredulity, suspected the cause, and wagged his head in something like self-mockery. While he'd always known this thing between him and Juby wasn't entirely rational, before Midge's bemused gaze he felt quite foolish. When next he spoke he went out of his way to sound more reasonable.

'All I'm saying, Midge, is that if you want to know what it was like in Rouklye, what it was *truly* like, I'm the one to ask, not Jube. To hear Juby talk, Rouklye was heaven on earth. Not a strand of honeysuckle out of place, sun always shining, workers singing happily in the fields, the full sepia scenario.

Well take it from me, kid, there was nothing "romantic" about the place. It was where we lived, that's all, day by day, year in, year out. I bet he hasn't mentioned the privations.'

'Privations?'

'No, course not. Cast a shadow on the soft-focus memory clips, that would. Dent the dewy-eyed illusion.'

'Not sure what you mean,' Midge said.

'I mean,' Edwin said, 'the "reality" of life there, then, real life, not retrospective fantasy life. Like having to walk to the only village pump for water, all weathers, and carry it home in buckets. No tap water, see. No electricity either. They had electricity up at The Big House and over at the rectory, but that was it, none for us plebs in the village or out Crowbarrow way. No flush toilets either, and let me tell you, my recent dive into old Crapper's masterpiece might not have made my day, but when it's working it's a hell of an advance on the filthy pit we had to use back then – and empty every few days with our own fair hands.'

He paused, perhaps expecting questions. None came. Unused to this side of him, the sharp tone, the bitterness, the best Midge could do was sit tight and hear him out.

So he continued.

'Listen to the Jubys of this world and you'll come away believing that if the Army hadn't given us the boot everything would be the same today as he seems to believe it was before, only with a symphonic soundtrack. Well it wouldn't, not by a long chalk. This isn't the Middle Ages.

Things don't stand still for centuries any more, even for decades. There wasn't some sort of preserving spell on the place. Rouklye wasn't excused by royal decree from time's march. If it hadn't been taken over by the government of the day there'd be new houses there now, with white UPVC doors, and satellite dishes wherever you looked, and there'd be a chippy or a kebab takeaway, and supermarket windows full of gaudy stickers; the rectory cottages would've been converted into "desirable residences" or second homes for the well-off, there'd be Porsches in Post Office Row, the church would have been bought by a firm of solicitors with a string of unbelievable names, and as for the old schoolhouse, my guess is it would be either a chic little restaurant or an organic tea shop with wholemeal scones and 26 varieties of herbal tea.'

He was on his hobby horse now, and cantering, eyes bright with the will to spill the true beans, and Midge had no choice but to sit there and hear him out.

'There'd be a pub too, of course. The nearest we got to a pub in Rouklye was some old boy, I forget his name, brewing ale in his parlor in return for a few pennies. Nowadays there'd be this yellow brick monstrosity, *The Cat and the Fiddle* or somesuch, for tourists to sit outside on summer evenings tossing crisp packets over their shoulders before driving back to their rented caravans on Gad Cliff, and every Saturday night gangs of tanked-up hooligans would be bellowing and singing at the top of their stupid voices and kicking lager cans into the village pond.'

He drew a long breath, and she thought he was done. But no, not quite.

'Has he said anything about the winters?'

'The winters?'

'That never seemed to end. The dense fogs, the furious storms, the rain. It rained for weeks sometimes in that valley. Turned the ground so soft you got mud round your ankles just strolling. And the cold. The sheer bloody blood-freezing cold, and the oh-so-long, pitch-black winter evenings, candles and flickering oil lamps our only light, bed early just to keep warm and because there was nothing to do.' He nodded at the little TV on his worktop. 'No telly then, Midge. No telly then.'

'No telly now, except here,' she said; a thought she'd not realized she'd expressed until it met a very sudden silence and Edwin's startled stare. But as he stared, his shoulders, which had been up somewhere round his ears during his rant, lowered, and his mouth twitched, and... he smiled.

'Thank you, Midge,' he said.

'Thank you?'

'For pricking my pomposity. I was doing a Juby. Filling your ears with my personal brand of bilge. "Roll up, folks, roll up, it's the Edwin Rainey Tripe Show!". Sorry, Midge. Sorry.'

'There's nothing to apologize for,' she said.

'Isn't there, though?'

'No. No. Your point of view, that's all.'

He laughed. 'My point of view. I like that. But you get its drift, that point of view?'

Rather than answer this, she said: 'If you feel like that about Rouklye...'

'Mm?'

'If you feel like that about the place why do you keep all those old photos?'

'Old photos?'

'The ones on the walls of my room.'

'Oh, those. My mum's. She was a bit of a photographer, traveled a lot in her youth. And later. Took photos in places I couldn't even find on the map. When the war came she set about photographing Rouklye and its environs in case it was bombed. It wasn't bombed, though it might as well have been given the end result. I framed some of her Rouklye prints after she died, hung then in the spare room, your room. Scattered a few of her old rocks in there too.'

'The rocks were hers?'

'Yeah, she was a geologist by profession.'

It hadn't so much as crossed her mind that the pictures and the rocks could have been her great-grandmother's, and she was amazed at her lack of perception. The chess set was hers, she'd known that, and the photos belonged more to her generation than Edwin's...

'Did your mother live here? This house?'

A short laugh. 'No. She didn't even stay in Dorset after

the evacuation. Stayed at her brother's in Huntingdonshire till the war ended, then off she went, on her travels. Hardly saw or heard from her for months on end. A whole year once. She was in her late seventies when she was killed.'

'Killed?'

'Mombasa, Kenya. The country's president had just died and some students celebrated by nicking a jeep, and a security officer fired at them. He missed the driver and hit my mother in the eye. The left one, I think. Died instantly, they said.'

'No one's ever told me about this,' Midge said.

'I told your mum when she was about your age, but she wasn't really interested – someone she never met, a country she knew nothing of – so she might not have thought to pass it on. Kristin was always more interested in the living, the present day.'

'Like Dad.'

'Yeah, like your dad. Peas in a pod, those two.'

'What was your mother doing in... where was it?'

'Mombasa. Not a clue. Never found out. She was always off somewhere in the world. Liked to be where things were buzzing or it felt like a buzz was imminent. That didn't include England most of the time. I don't take after her. Real stay-at-home, me, always was.'

'Tell me more about growing up in Rouklye,' Midge said.

He eyed her suspiciously. 'Why? To compare my version with Juby's?'

She fidgeted uncomfortably, leaving no doubt that he wasn't far wrong. Nevertheless, he obliged.

'For Juby,' he said, 'there was nowhere like it. Me either till I hit my teens. Nothing to compare it with, you see. There wasn't much in the way of transport then, so we rarely left the valley. We played and we wandered and larked about for miles without fear, hunted rabbit, pheasant, fished more or less wherever we wanted, raided orchards...'

He sat back in his chair.

'Sounds good, doesn't it? And it was, if you were young, innocent, kept your nose relatively clean. We had a lot more freedom than today's kids, that's for sure, but it was an illusory freedom. Rouklye was pretty much a feudal set-up, going back centuries. The village and most of the valley belonged to the Flemings at the Big House and everyone was subservient to them, working for them, living there by their good graces, patronage, whatever you want to call it. Whenever the Squire strolled by in his nice shooting jacket, with his smart walking stick, whenever he came by, lesser men – which was all of 'em – would doff their caps or tug their forelocks, and – '

'You're talking a foreign language,' Midge said.

' – and the kids would suddenly be on their best behavior 'cos they were told to be or else, whenever he was about, and some of the women even *curtsied*, for God's sake. Not my mum, though. Lisette Rainey curtsied neither to man nor beast – specially man.' He chuckled at this, paused, then said: 'They weren't a bad lot for their class, the Flemings, but you were never in much doubt where you stood in life's pecking order. Even in church they had their own pews away from us peasants. Church! The supreme defender of the hierarchy principle was the Rector. A beast of a man, very full of himself, boomed the scriptures from the pulpit on Sunday and off-duty strutted about in plus-fours scowling at youngsters and working people. He carried a tasseled leather dog whip and didn't hesitate to use it, not always on dogs. Lashed me with it once for smirking as he passed by. When Mum saw the marks she went after him, cracked him across the head with a broom handle and asked him how he liked it. He never touched me again.' *

'I think I would have liked *her*,' Midge said. 'Your mum.'

Edwin smiled. 'The old bat had her moments. But this knowing your place thing. When we boys saw the squire sweeping the countryside with his binoculars we thought he was keeping an eye on us to make sure we weren't up to no good. Fact is, he was a keen bird-watcher and probably not bothered about us at all. But that wasn't the point. No, the *point* was that it was his land and he had the right to tick us off, march us home, even demand that we were given a good hiding if it suited him. As we got older that started to get to some of us. A couple of my mates left the village when they

---

* To meet Lisette Rainey, Edwin's redoubtable mother, and learn of the devastating event that followed her move to her brother Ned's house, see *The Rainey Seasons*, published by 8N Publishing.

were old enough, got jobs outside, and when I was fourteen I followed their lead. Then I felt free, even though I had to mind my ps and qs with my boss and work longer hours than anyone should have to for such a pittance.'

Midge caught a movement outside, a shadow crossing one of the opaque white blinds. A movement and a shadow which Edwin, caught up in his lecture, missed.

'I wasn't in Rouklye when the order to quit came. Juby still was. Working part-time at the farm, I think. Most people left without fuss, and it didn't take some very long to realize that there was a lot to be said for the mod cons they hadn't had before. Some profited in other ways too. There were more soldiers about, and they spent well – specially the yanks when they were here in the early days – and a few of them started families with local lasses. Before you knew it, the military had become part of the community, and...'

Another movement outside, which, this time, he noticed. A small creak of something touching wood: a hand perhaps, or an ear. Edwin put a finger to his lips, eased himself out of his chair, and crept, Tom-and-Jerry like, to the door. When he gave it a thump with the side of his fist, there was a small yelp on the other side, and footsteps scurrying away.

He returned to his chair, settled back, legs stretched out before him. 'Where was I?'

'Some people preferred life outside Rouklye.'

'Yes. Right. But Juby wasn't one of them. For him, there was nothing to touch Rouklye. Nowhere. There was a reason for that, of course. I mean he wasn't really one of us.'

He gave her the kind of look that seeks to share an amused confidence about the person under discussion; a confidence Midge found herself unwilling to share. Mildly indignant on Juby's behalf, she said: 'Why should he be one of you? What's so wrong with being an individual and liking the place you were born and grew up in?'

Edwin's eyebrows rose until they weren't far short of where his hairline had been when he was twenty-five.

'What the hell's the old twit been telling you now?'

'He just tells me what it was like there as he remembers it. He doesn't make out that it was all perfect the way you think he does. He has some good memories, that's all.'

The eyebrows returned to their usual level as he pondered her words. Then he said: 'You know, I think...'

'What do you think?' Midge asked when he left the rest hanging.

He drew his legs in, levered himself out of the chair, squared his shoulders, and adjusted his feet in such a way that she expected him to embark on one of his impressions: of a penguin perhaps. But he didn't do a penguin, he did an Edwin Rainey, strolling in a wholly ordinary way to the workbench, where he leant on his elbows next to her, looking intently at the broken helicopter.

'I think we should see what can be done about this.'

18

More relaxed in Inger's company since she'd spent time with her away from Edwin, Juby and Underthorpe, Midge worked cheerfully enough in the shop the morning after the trip to Weymouth. She smiled more than usual and was more confident when dealing with customers. But the afternoon was quiet, and Inger insisted that she spend some of it in the back garden 'where the sun is', reading a collection of stories that she recommended. Sitting under a sycamore in a creaky old deckchair, Midge at first enjoyed her garden exile, but grew restless after an hour – the stories didn't sufficiently fire her imagination – and went indoors and up to her room. There, she cast about for something to do or look at, and her gaze settled on the book of poems, *On the Bleak Ridge*, and as it did so she recalled Inger's thoughts about used books having histories. She picked the book up. 'Okay,' she said, 'so what's your backstory then?'

She turned the book over, looked inside the front and back flaps, hoping for information that she hadn't bothered to seek previously, but there was nothing of use: on one flap a note about the little Alabama publishing house, on the other a few lines stating that the poems were the work of an English poet.

'Oh, so you're English,' she said. 'Well now, what's *your* history, William Rainey? Who are you, or were you, and am I related to you?' *

She opened the book then, and read a few of the poems, at speed, silently, as though racing through an article or letter. Any likelihood of her getting something out of poetry at some future date was scotched at school when the class was told to learn a number of poems – old ones mostly – and recite them, individually, standing in front of everyone else. She didn't care for many of those prehistoric verses, but at least most of them rhymed, while few of the Rainey poems did. She wasn't sure if many of his even *qualified* as poems. They looked right – the way they were laid out, uneven lines, eccentric spacing and all – but most of them read like diary notes, or someone bitching about something, or commenting on the weather, or... life.

Determined to make an attempt to 'appreciate' them, or whatever it was you were supposed to do with poems, she turned a page at random, where she found one called *The Circle*, which she read aloud, slowly, carefully.

We each took a step backward,
As though quitting a circle
We'd been caught occupying by mistake.

Old identities had no place here.

---

* Everything there is to know about William Rainey can be found in the third volume of this sequence, *The Silence of Bleakridge* (8N Publishing).

And in the wink of an eye
They were lost to us, the people we'd known,
The places we'd lived in and visited,

The hopes, the joys, the whole caboodle.

Not a whisper remained of past events,
Of sights or sounds or incidents.
Like lost souls we moved off on the long road.

The stars were very bright.

She sighed – Now what was *that* supposed to be about? – and set the book aside.

While it had felt like an inconsequential, even wasted day, in the evening something unexpected happened. Unexpected and rather pleasing. She was in the kitchen with Inger, footling about, moving small things around for the sake of it, and Edwin had just come downstairs and opened his mouth to say something, when a light knock on the back door drew him in its direction instead. He opened the door and there followed a brief exchange of words on the step, at the conclusion of which he brought Juby in – Juby waving a bottle of Scotch.

What they talked about in the hour or so of Juby's visit Midge couldn't have said afterwards, but it wasn't dull talk and she didn't feel in any way excluded from it or by it. Her age and limited experience of life made some difference, of course, but to her more than the others, it seemed. Juby and her grandparents were quite strong personalities while she, by her own estimation, was a shallow, colorless creature with few opinions of value. While giving a proffered glass of the Scotch a miss, she tried to look bright and nod in all the right places, and offer contributions when invited, and they seemed to welcome this, as though they genuinely valued her input. At a certain point during the evening she came to the conclusion that she really liked these people, all three of them, different as they were from one another. She realized something else too. That they liked her. In their assembled company she felt like a fourth member of a charmed quartet.

Curiously, Edwin no longer seemed to bear Juby any ill will. Had clearing the air with her made some sort of difference then? Be good to think that that was the reason they seemed so friendly tonight. As he was leaving, Juby offered his hand to Edwin and Edwin shook it. Juby nodded, just once, and Edwin nodded once in return, a pair of identical question-and-answer gestures that said 'All right?' and 'All right,' but spoke, or seemed to speak, volumes.

'Can't remember when I last saw them so chummy,' Inger whispered to Midge. 'Must be your influence.'

'Mine? I haven't done anything.'

Inger gave her shoulders a squeeze, but added nothing.

Up in her room, in the third letter she planned to post in

a few days' time, Midge told Nessa about the evening. 'I'M AN INFLUENCE!', she crowed. It was late, so it was not a long letter, but she envied her friend all the news she would read on her return and looked forward to filling in the gaps when she too was back home. So often when they were together she sat or walked quietly within the arc of Nessa's easy charm while hearing of this or that discovery, insight, passing fancy. Ness would inevitably have loads to tell her about her holiday, but for once, surely, it would be she, Midge, who would have the really fascinating tale to tell. Whatever she'd experienced or observed in Scotland, Ness would have met no one like Juby Bench, been nowhere as odd as Rouklye, and certainly not experienced a phenomenon like the almost-there boy. She considered her accumulating news. What if nothing else happened and she'd already put the best bits in the letters? If that were the case, there'd be nothing much to add when she and Nessa met. Maybe she should hold back on future info; merely hint that stuff was happening. Yes. That way she stood a chance of keeping her friend enthralled while she talked. What a reversal *that* would be!

19

The sun lay like a golden carpet all along the street. It was just after lunch and she was outside, tidying the rack of second-hand books that Inger put there most days in hope of attracting passers-by. A reflection caught her eye in the window: Juby, stooping out of the doorway of The Ferryman. She saw him glance her way, hesitate, then cross the road, his great black jacket flapping around him as though about to bear him up, up and away.

'Another hott'un, Evy.'

She half turned. He looked tired, all lines and furrows, even more than at breakfast the other morning.

'Yep. Late today, aren't you?'

'Yeah, couldn't seem to get the old bones off the mattress.' He bent down to inspect the rack. 'Still using you as slave-labor, is she?'

'I'm just passing the time. Trish is here, so I'm not really needed.'

'Trish?'

'She comes in to help out a couple days a week.'

'Even though you're here?'

'Regular arrangement. You going to Rouklye again?'

'Mm. Just off.'

She watched him fingering the spines of the books, tried to imagine him at sixteen, when he must have looked so like the almost-there boy. Could the boy be him? The ghost of Juby as a lad? Could you have a ghost (or whatever you want to call it) of someone who wasn't dead, a specter of them at an earlier point in their life? If so, was he trying to

142

communicate with her from the past for some reason? Well, next time she'd be looking out for him, ready for him.

'Whoa, haven't seen this for a while.' Juby pulled a paperback from the rack. 'Last read this in me twenties. Read it three times back then.'

'What is it?' Midge asked.

He held it up and she read the title – *Last and First Men* – and the author's name: Olaf Stapledon. She'd never heard of him or the book.

Juby flipped the pages, all the way to the last, read the closing paragraph, and smiled. 'That line,' he said. 'Always remembered that line. Just add a tiny little "a" to it and it becomes completely personal.'

'I'm sure Gran will let you have it,' Midge said.

Juby looked up. 'Uh?'

'If you want it. Or you could buy it. It's very cheap.'

He closed the book, returned it to the shelf, straightened up, and tapped the side of his head. 'Like most things,' he said, 'the bits I want are all in here,' but he didn't move for a while after saying this, as though held in place by a thought that wouldn't quite let go of him.

In the lull, Midge said: 'I could go with you again.'

This seemed to shake him out of his reverie, for he focused on her, in a confused sort of way.

'Uh?'

'We needn't rush about,' she added.

'What are you talking about?'

'You're going to Rouklye again. I thought I might go too.'

'You've seen it. Most of it.'

'I don't mind seeing it again.'

He squinted down at her as though trying to make up his mind about something, then, slowly, said: 'You know, Evy, there's something about you.'

'Something...?'

'Something I can't quite put my f...' He shook his head as if to dismiss the puzzle, and said: 'You'll have to get permission.'

'Permission?'

'Like last time. To go with me.'

'All right,' she said. 'I'll ask Gran.'

'No. Edwin this time.'

'Why him?'

'Because that's the way it's got to be.'

He would wait in The Ferryman car park for fifteen minutes, he said. If she wasn't there by the end of that time he would go without her. He crossed the street and Midge went into the shop. Trish was sorting books and Inger was flicking through publishers' catalogues.

'Juby says I can go to Rouklye with him again if it's all right,' she said.

'You'll have to ask Edwin,' Inger said.

'I was going to. Where is he?'

'That stupid hidey-hole of his.'

She went down the garden and pressed an ear to the

144

door of the Pottering Shed. The distant sound of a muted cricket commentary, the thwack of leather on willow, the roar of a crowd constrained by the small speakers of his portable television turned low. She knocked. A startled crash from inside, then the cricket commentary was silenced.

'Who's there? Friend or Viking?'

'Midge.'

The door opened to reveal an eye and half a nose. The eye explored the space around her, saw that she was alone, and the door opened a fraction more to make room for a second eye and the rest of the nose.

'Wanna come in?'

'No, I just have to ask if...'

She hesitated, worried that he would hit the roof.

'Talk to me, Midge, talk to me, the West Indies are beating the bails off England in here.'

'Promise you won't be annoyed.'

'Me, annoyed? When am I ever annoyed?'

'When I go to Rouklye with Juby.'

Edwin's brows knitted together in the small space provided.

'What the heck's so fascinating about a bunch of old ruins?'

'I won't if you don't want me to,' she said.

'Are you asking my leave?'

'He says I must.'

Amazement filled the eyes in the doorway. 'He told you

to ask me?' She nodded. 'Well whaddayaknow.'

'It'll be all right,' she said. 'Really. And...'

'And what?'

'It is only a point of view.'

Edwin gave a hoot of laughter; then: 'If I say yes, one favor in return.'

'What's that?'

'Take it all with a very large pinch of sea salt.'

'That's it?' she said.

'That's it.'

He shut the door without waiting for her agreement, and once again Midge accompanied Juby to Rouklye – with no idea that she would learn something today that would make this August as memorable as any in her entire life, past or future.

20

On the way, Midge, thinking about the second-hand, now third-hand, book of poems in her room, asked her driver if he knew of any other Raineys.

'Raineys as in wet weather or people?' he said.

'You know what I mean.'

'The only Raineys I ever knew were Ed and his mum.'

'Back in old Rouklye.'

'Back in *living* Rouklye. *Unruined* Rouklye.'

'Didn't Ed… Grandpa… have any brothers or sisters?'

'No.'

'Aunts, uncles, cousins?'

'If he did I never met them or heard of them.'

'What about his dad? Wasn't he there?'

'Ah, well, Ed's dad… long story. Or short one, depending who tells it. But no, he wasn't there.'

'His name wasn't William, was it?'

'I don't remember his name. Probably never heard it. Where'd you get William from?'

'Oh, it doesn't matter.'

'No?'

'No, not really.'

'Now that I think of it,' Juby said, 'I did meet a William once.'

'Oh yes? A particular William, or…?'

'A William Rainey. Long time ago. Forty-four, I think.'

'Forty-four what?'

'The year. 1944. Or early forty-five. He can't have been much older than I was at the time. Two years, three, four.'

'Who was he?' Midge asked.

'He was a squaddie.'

'A what?'

'Squaddie. Soldier. Ordinary soldier, not an officer.'

'You mean he was in the Army?'

'Well, unless it was fancy dress.'

'Where'd you meet him?'

'Rouklye.'

'Hang on now, wait,' Midge said. 'Didn't the Army move into Rouklye once all the people had gone?'

'Yes.'

'So why was a soldier there at the same time you were?'

'I snuck back in one day,' Juby said. 'Managed not to be seen by the uniforms till I came across him – in my house.'

'Your house? What was he doing there?'

'Doodling. On one of the walls. I wasn't too happy about that.'

'No, I'm sure, but... you didn't live there any more.'

'No, and whose fault was that? The bloody Army's.'

'This solider. What did he do when he saw you?'

'He stopped his doodling.'

'No, I mean if you weren't supposed to be there?'

'As I remember it, he was skiving. Taking time out. Keeping his head down. We chatted for a bit, then parted company.'

'Yeah, but the name. Rainey.'

He glanced at her. 'It's just that, Evy, a name, and his happened to be Rainey. Didn't make him a relation, though it's probably the reason I remember him after all this time. I mean the name and him being a soldier, and meeting him in Rouklye of all places. Quite a combination.'

A few minutes later they turned off the road, onto the track that took them between fields, past the MoD signs and barbed wire fencing and many a padlocked gate, down to Rouklye, where they took a sharp left at the corner of Post Office Row, to the broad expanse of ground that served as the car park.

There weren't many vehicles there. Early yet for visitors. Juby parked near the cluster of trees above the pond where, for the moment, there was a limited canopy of shade.

After a shaky start it was turning into the kind of summer that many dream about, dress down for, and complain about if it lasts for more than a few days. In parts of the country water companies were threatening to ration supplies, in Yorkshire and Somerset hosepipe bans were already in force, and beaches were packed solid with brown and red bodies. Visitors to Rouklye who fancied a spot of sea air had to trek out to Crowbarrow on foot, but there, though they could sprawl on the sand and shingle and dip their toes in the water, they could not, as they might elsewhere, rent deckchairs and powerboats, or buy icecreams and fizzy drinks, buckets and spades. This was Ministry of Defense property, after all, not a holiday resort.

In Post Office Row a pair of paint-flecked ladders leant against the inner walls of one of the cottages as two workmen filled in gaps in stonework and between bricks. Juby stood watching them for a minute, then went next door. Midge did not follow him. She no longer felt obliged to go wherever he did, and doubted that he expected her to. Not having known these buildings when they were whole and in daily use she could not share his nostalgia for them, but it was curious: each time she came here she was a bit more intrigued by the place and the people who'd lived here. She had no trouble taking Edwin's advice about Juby's view of the old days in Rouklye, but, mildly charmed by that view, she saw no reason to discard it completely.

And there was something else: the voices, which seemed clearer today. There seemed to be more of them too. She could hear them within the shell of the old post office, though when she went in they retreated a little, as if stepping back into their true realm of residency. She listened hard, wished she could make out what they said, but a clarity-denying barrier stood between her and the voices. They didn't alarm her, the voices; worried her no more than the occasional movement at the corner of her eye worried her. Movements which, when confronted, revealed nothing at all.

When Juby again led the way down to his former house, she discovered that his purpose was no longer merely to gaze and remember. 'Made some headway yesterday,' he told her, fishing a pair of secateurs from his trouser pocket. 'Make a bit more today, and tomorrow, with any luck, I'll be through.'

'You're trying to get to the house?' she said.

'Sssh, voice down, trees are probably bugged. Keep a look-out.'

He plunged into the undergrowth, leaving her a startled guard at the perimeter.

'But the signs,' she hissed. 'They say it's unsafe.'

'Whole damn world's unsafe,' Juby grunted. 'Take note of every sign and you never do a thing. Eyes peeled now.'

Peeled eyes darting all over the place, she did her best not to look like a partner-in-crime, pretending merely to have paused to admire the towering weeds. To mask the clip-clip-clip of the secateurs, she began whistling a catchy little song she disliked, though the odd passer-by still glanced curiously at her. After some minutes of this she got fed up and, choosing her moment, went in after Juby. Something sharp tore her arm, introducing a quick red line to the flesh. She saw scratches on Juby's arms too, but, intent on his task, he seemed unaware of them. He was indeed closer to the house than the last time she'd come here with him, but today's efforts did not take him all the way, as he'd hoped, the secateurs proving inadequate against heavy-duty barbed-wire.

'Fool,' he growled, 'gotta be tomorrow now,' adding, just under his breath: 'Given the time.'

Rouklye church was the only building Juby had shown no inclination to visit while she was with him, but today, as he loitered in the shade of the King's oak, she noticed him inching toward the steps, furtively, as though the movement were beyond his control or notice. Faintly amused by this, she seized the initiative, bounded up them, and at the top, in the unusual position of being taller than Juby Bench, said:

'Coming?'

He frowned up at her. 'Coming?'

'To the church.'

'The church? Me?'

'Yeah, let's take a look.'

'I wouldn't bother,' he said. 'It's all fake in there.'

'Fake?'

'Most of the original furnishings went long ago, the bells and the old organ were moved to a church a few miles away, and the pulpit that'd been there since God knows when was moved to the Army base at Ralworth.'

'How do you know all this if you have no interest in the place?' Midge asked.

'I've read stuff. Read and heard. Whatever furniture's in there now – pews, pulpits, all the other holy stuff – it's either new or brought in from other churches so the Army can be patted on the back for making it look good, conveniently keeping quiet about it being hit a couple of times by their own shells.'

'Okay. But I want to take a look anyway.'

A disapproving sound deep in his throat, but when she turned away he took the first step up, then the next, the next, the next, slowly, grudgingly, and before long stood a yard or so from her, at the top, looking about him. Elsewhere the grass was browned and stunted from weeks of sunshine, an almost complete absence of rain, but up here the turf was as green as could be. Heavily-corroded iron crosses dotted among headstones were so immaculate that they might have been there no time at all, though the dates chiseled into them belied this.

'They send squaddies to scrub them with wire brushes,' Juby said of the headstones. 'Water the grass too. Mustn't let the public think they've let the *church* go, whatever the fuck else. Excuse my Swedish.'

'I didn't know that was Swedish,' she said, and set off toward the church. Along the way, she glanced with little interest at two of the headstones, but paused at a third.

WILLIAM LEONARD BROOKER
Beloved Son of Rouklye
Born Here 1904, Mourned Here 1919

Well, well. Billy Brooker. She'd seen a photo of him as a boy of about eight, the remnants of the house in which he might have uttered his first cry and was probably laid out aged fifteen, and here she was now, standing at his final resting place. She sighed, without quite knowing why, and moved on.

The heavy oak door of the church stood ajar. She slipped inside, to a world where shadows clung to some walls and sunlight, streaming through colored glass, splashed others and brought a glow to the mellow wood of pews and lecterns. A young couple in shorts and canvas shoes picked a reverent way through an enormous leather-bound bible with faded gold tooling. Three elderly ladies selected picture postcards from a revolving rack that squealed at every turn, dipping into their purses for coins to drop in the 'honesty box'. A notice behind the rack told how some of the original stained glass had been smashed after the evacuation (whether by intent or accident was not made clear) and other panels removed for preservation elsewhere, along with the three-sided Jacobean pulpit and a mighty old pipe-organ that had stood in the chancel. Replacement furniture and artifacts had been brought in since the church was restored and reopened to the public – as a curiosity, not for worship or any of the other traditional purposes.

Midge gazed about her. Clean and cared-for as it was, the place lacked everything it must once have had, not least that musty, leathery, waxy smell of accumulated centuries. Abandoned for decades, then done up to be offered to the public as a perfect exhibit among ruins, it felt wrong.

For her, the main points of interest were the boards fixed to one of the whitewashed walls: the information panels that Inger had told her about. The first things to catch her eye were two small posters advertising auctions of farm equipment, tools, utensils, furniture and livestock. Both were held in December 1943, one on the 9th, the other on the 14th, just days before the evacuation. From these she moved along the exhibits step by slow step, examining as she went sepia and black-and-white photographs, notes, letters, printed and hand-written documents, all of them relevant in one way or another to the Rouklye Valley of the years before the official decree that terminated its history. She was drawn to a set of prints showing Crowbarrow properties and scenes and some of the people who'd lived and worked there. In one of these, dated 1936, a bunch of fishermen were sorting a heavy mackerel catch on the beach. They might not all have been Millers, but it seemed likely to her that some were. In captions below these pictures a number of their subjects were named. One or more of these might have been forebears of hers, but she had no way of knowing which or who they might be.

While recognizing the names of some of the Millers Juby had listed on their walk to Crowbarrow, one that she was sure he hadn't mentioned caught her eye. It belonged to a narrow-shouldered woman in a long apron who sat outside a cottage repairing a fishing basket while her husband stood beside her, staring at the camera. According to the information provided, the man was Jack Miller and his wife's name was Miggie. Miggie? Was that where her own name came from: the nickname she'd had since she was very small? Could this woman be her great *grandmother*? She peered closely at Miggie Miller's face. Was there any likeness between this long-gone woman and her? If there was, she couldn't see it, but the woman was very old. She read the note below the photo.

> Jack and Miggie Miller, evacuated from
> Crowbarrow in December 1943, moved to a
> very neglected house at Langton, where they

endured extremes of damp and cold in great discomfort without complaint. Jack fell victim to bronchitis soon after the war, but Miggie, crippled with arthritis, lived until 1959, aged 94, her gallant spirit undefeated and her quick tongue uncurbed. She was a generous, warm-hearted neighbor and a faithful friend whose memory is treasured by old inhabitants of Rouklye and Crowbarrow.

Not the Millers that went to America then, Midge thought.

One of the smaller displays was devoted to the Brooker family, with a photo of Billy himself as the centerpiece. He looked about fourteen in this, a graceless lad holding a pail of milk in each hand. His mother and father smiled out of another picture with their daughters, May, Rosie and Sarah.

Saddened to have met Billy's family on a shadowy interior wall after reading his epitaph in the brilliant light outside, Midge was about to turn away when a voice, close behind her, said: 'There we are!'

She jumped. 'I didn't hear you come in,' she said.

'Handsome pair, weren't we?' Juby said.

He reached past her and tapped a print with a fingernail. She hadn't missed the picture, but, not reading the caption, had failed to connect the people in it with anyone she knew. Looking properly now, she recognized, vaguely, Edwin and

Juby in their early teens, the one squat and beaming, the other lanky and fidgety (looking very much like the almost-there boy), standing with a tall confident woman with untidy hair who stared intently as if daring the photographer to include her in such nonsense. The caption read: 'Miss L.M. Rainey with son Edward and friend Joey'.

Juby sighed. 'Edward and Joey.'

'Makes you wonder how many other names are... wrong.'

She'd glanced at him, and started. He was peering at the photo through old-fashioned glasses, really old-fashioned ones, with round lenses, gold frame.

'You're wearing glasses,' she said, rather obviously.

He looked at her. 'Me? Glasses?'

'Are you saying they're not glasses?'

He fingered the frame. 'They're my specs.'

'Specs, glasses, same difference.'

'I only wear them to look at things close-up.'

'Not for driving then.'

'No reason to wear 'em for driving. I can see the nose of the car without 'em.'

'I think you're meant to see a bit further than the car's nose,' she said.

'Oh, wow! Found some!'

For the second time in thirty seconds or less, Midge gave a small startled jump, turning the other way to find, inches from hers, the face if a woman with spiky red hair staring at a photo. Noticing the jump, the woman quickly apologized.

'Sorry. Sorry. Got a little excited there. But look!' She pointed to the caption beneath the photo of young Juby and Edwin with Edwin's mother. 'Rainey. My mom's name before she married Dad. I'm here on vacation, see, trying to track down any relatives of hers. Old relatives, that is, past relatives. I heard about this place – Rowk-lie...?'

'*Rook*-lee,' Midge said.

'Yeah, right, I heard there were Raineys here that settled in America and hey, well, here's two of them!' Her face glowed as she read the names. 'Miss L.M. Rainey and son Edward. I don't know an L.M. Rainey, or an Edward, but...' – she scanned the other boards – 'they seem to be the only Raineys here, so maybe it's them that went and started my mom's branch of the family.'

She glanced again at Midge, then at Juby, who'd taken his glasses off and stepped back a pace.

'Alana,' she said. 'Florence, Alabama.'

'Alana-Florence-Alabama?' Midge said.

The woman chuckled. 'Sorry, never get it right over here. Florence, Alabama's where I'm from, where I reside these days, anyhow. Alana's my *name*. Alana Mildren. Mildren's my husband's name.'

'Shall we go?' Juby said to Midge.

'I don't suppose you know anything about these people, do you?' Alana said, tapping the photo.

'No,' Juby said.

'I ask because this young man...' she glanced at Juby and

touched the teenage image of him, 'well, he does kinda resemble you. No relation, are you?'

'No,' Juby said again.

'And Edward, Edward Rainey, know anything of him?'

This time Juby merely grunted, and headed for the door. Midge, embarrassed, said 'Good to meet you,' and went after him. He was already outside when she reached the door, and she was about to follow when she saw a sheet of paper taped to the back of the door – a photocopy, she later learnt, of a hand-written note pinned there by one of the residents as everyone as leaving that December of 1943.

Please treat the church and houses with care.
We have given up our homes, where many of
us have lived for generations, to help win the
war and keep men free. We shall return one day
and thank you for treating the village kindly.

She found Juby standing well away from the nearest crosses and headstones in an arc of sunshine between the mottled shadows of overhanging boughs.

'Why didn't you tell that woman that you knew Grandpa and his mother?' she asked.

'A name-tourist,' he growled. 'No time for 'em.'

'She might be a relative via her mother. I knew about the Millers who went to America from here, but nothing of any

Raineys. Are you sure you didn't know any others?'

'I'm sure.'

'Maybe there were some before your time and they were the ones that went. Hey, I might have Rainey relatives back home that I don't even know about.' She laughed, a bit sourly. 'Unknown Millers here, unknown Raineys there.'

Juby, no longer listening. tapped a sandaled foot on a bright patch of grass. 'This is it,' he said.

Midge looked down. 'This is what?'

'Where I want to lie.'

'Lie? Meaning...?'

'Good view from here. Of what's left anyway. Not that I expect to be sitting up and looking very often.'

He chuckled rather absently as he said this, and as he raised his eyes from the bright clipped grass the light caught them in such a way that for a small cluster of instants, from where Midge stood it was like looking through his skull, to empty sky behind him. Gray sky. But then he turned his head, just a fraction, and the emptiness was gone, and his eyes were on her, as he said her name – 'Evy' – very quietly.

'Yes?' she said.

'Evy,' he said again, a little louder.

'What?'

'Would you say that we're friends, you and me?'

'Friends?'

It was as unexpected as any question could be. Friends? With him? Friends were people your own age who you could relax with, not weird old men who hung around ruins and hated authority and churches. And she'd only met him a few days ago. How could you be friends with someone this ancient who you hardly knew? But there was only one answer to such a direct question, with such eyes upon you.

'I... think so.'

'Good. 'Cos I need to tell you something and I'd rather tell it to a friend.'

She waited, wondering.

'Back in January,' he said slowly, hesitated, and started again. 'Back in January I went to the quack's. Hadn't been feeling right for a while. Chest pains, palpitations, giddy spells. He did some tests and when the results came back he called me in. Told me I had six months.'

'Six months?' she said. 'What for?' And immediately realized her foolishness.

'Six months maximum. Be lucky to see July, he said.'

'July? But it's...'

'August, yeah. So I'm lucky after all. Or stubborn. Had to hang on till they opened up for the month. Nearly didn't make it. I was a bit poorly, but I made myself get up, drove hell for leather till I was within sight of the hills. Perked up no end then. Coming home does that to a fella.'

It was probably the most appalling news she'd ever heard first-hand – even worse than hearing that her great-grandmother had been killed by a stray bullet in Africa. That had happened so long ago, to someone she'd never known, but this, here, right now, Juby Bench...

'It could happen any time,' he said. 'Any minute, no predicting, except that it won't be long. That's why I'm in Rouklye every day. Don't want to die in the car, or me bed at The Ferryman.'

'You mean you want to die in *Rouklye*?' she said. 'But...'

'But what?'

'But you can't!'

'I can't die?'

'Can't die *here*.'

'There's nowhere else I'd rather,' he said.

'What about the other day? That cliff we climbed. I thought it was a bit of a strain for you, but...'

She puffed her cheeks out in astonished dismay.

'I just wanted to walk up there one last time,' he said. 'Day after day, I look on everything I do and see here as for the last time. Soon it will be.'

'What about your family in Sweden? Shouldn't you be with them?'

'What, when I turn up my toes?' A curt shake of the head. 'I don't want an audience. I've said my goodbyes there.'

'Oh, they know then?'

'No, I just said goodbye, but with special care, so they'll remember afterwards. You're the only one I've told.'

'But why me?' she said. 'Why not Gran?'

'Why you? Because you're like me.'

'Like you?'

'You feel for this place. And you hear things.'

'Hear things?'

'Footsteps? Whispers? Chatter? The odd little laugh?'

She took a breath. 'How'd you know?'

'Just a guess.'

'You mean you hear them too?'

'Sometimes. Not much this trip, but sometimes.'

'Why do you believe that I hear such things?'

'Oh, the way you look sometimes.'

'The way I look?'

'The odd little smile. A sideways glance at nothing. That's why I say you're like me. Rare birds, you and me, Evy. Rare birds.'

She turned her head. Gazed past the schoolhouse to the woods in which the ruins of his house and several others stood. 'So there *are* ghosts here,' she murmured.

'Ghosts?'

'Not that I *believe* in ghosts.'

'Could be something else,' he said.

'Something else?'

'Like, well, I dunno, a small part of some of those that used to live here, the ones that really didn't want to go. They might still be alive somewhere, no inkling that a bit of them – spirit, soul, whatever – hangs about here still, in a quiet sort of way.'

'Are you serious?' she said.

The question seemed to embarrass him. 'No. Nah. It's

just… I don't know.'

'Well, something like that might explain the boy…'

'Boy? What boy?'

'He could be you as you were the day you left. The you that didn't want to go. He must be about the age you were then.'

'Are you telling me,' Juby said slowly, 'that you've seen me here – as a lad?'

'He has to be you. He looked like the you in that picture in the church.'

He was frankly amazed. 'I never see people. Never have. Just… get a sense of them.' But then he laughed, with real, untrammeled amusement. 'A young me! Wooh! And you *see* me? Clearly?'

'Clear as day. Not often, but…' She stopped. There was more pressing business. 'Can we get back to the other thing?'

'Other thing?'

'You. Now. And what's going to happen.'

The gravity of this flooded back. 'You mustn't tell anyone,' he said. 'No one, even Inger. I don't want people being careful what they say around me or feeling sorry for me. I'm only telling you because I want you to do something.'

'Do something? Me? What could I do?'

'I want you to see that they put me here.' He tapped his foot on his chosen plot. 'Right here. I want no service, mind. No prayers or hymns or what-have-you. No Holy Joe in a starched frock spouting his dust-to-dust shit over a bit of cheap pine. Promise me, girl. I'm counting on...' He stopped. 'What's up? What is it?'

The air, the hot unmoving air, had quivered, or felt as if it had, and Midge was staring past him, a little to one side of him. Following her lead, Juby half turned, looked round, but only she could see the boy standing there. The almost-there boy. The boy saw her too, and the look on his face was so desperately sad that she almost cried out.

Juby darted a questioning glance at her, and when she nodded he did a very odd thing. Having learned where the boy was he turned and walked straight through him, whereupon the lad jumped, like someone woken sharply from a dream, and vanished.

21

Next morning, following a fitful night of fragmented dreams in which Juby Bench played a prominent part, there was a letter from Nessa. While congratulating herself for having slipped the Underthorpe address through her friend's door before coming away, Midge was surprised to learn the Friedmans were home already until she read why. Nessa's aunt, who lived a few doors down from them, had been diagnosed with ovarian cancer and needed comforting – especially, Ness confided, since her boyfriend had cleared off a few days before she received the news. All this was delivered in a handful of lines. The rest of the letter was bubbly and chatty, full of the holiday in Scotland, what she'd bought, boys she'd fancied – shallow stuff to Midge, whose mind bore a banner headline beside which such news, even that of the aunt's illness, was inconsequential in the extreme.

Juby's going to die.

Her room wasn't directly opposite his at The Ferryman, but she could see his window well enough to tell if the curtains were drawn. Last night they had been, but now they were pulled back, which meant that he'd probably polished off his Full English and already driven to Rouklye, to start his day there. What a dismal scenario! To go to a particular place to await your death, terrified of being somewhere else when it came.

She picked up Nessa's letter again. Reading it a second time might take her mind off Juby. Her eyes skated down the page and fell off the end, having taken nothing in. She returned the letter to the tray Edwin had left outside her door with a discreet knock. Warm rolls, apricot jam, hot chocolate. Breakfast in bed. They'd never done that before. Perhaps they didn't fancy looking at her miserable mug over the kitchen table.

'Miserable mug,' she said to the mirror. 'Miserable, lousy, stinking, *useless* mug!'

Mirror Midge glared back at her, clearly agreeing, and non-mirror Midge turned away. There was nothing for it, nothing at all, but to sit tight and wait for 'it' to happen. But then what? Go to Army High Command or whatever the hell they were called, and say, 'Excuse me, chaps, Juby Bench wants to be buried in Rouklye, follow me, I'll show you where'?

Is that the way he imagined it? Did he honestly think they'd listen to her? You had to be off your trolley to believe shit like that.

Was that it? Was Juby mad? Well, what if he was? He was still someone whose friend she'd claimed to be when pressed, and it was she – she and no one else – that he'd entrusted with his terrible secret. Sometime today or tomorrow or the day after he might sit down suddenly in the schoolhouse or under George V's oak, struggling for breath, and know that this was it. Or, on the track to Crowbarrow under yet another blistering sun, he might keel over and lie there till a range warden drove up and covered his face with a rough Army blanket and radioed for a truck or something to take him away. He might even breathe his last in the spiraling, dust-flecked sunlight of the old post office, on the weed-infested floor that smelt of nettles and moss, while visitors took pictures as though death were part of the show.

The worst of it was that there was no one she could talk to about it. Not even Inger. Tears stung her eyes. She dashed them angrily away. Don't be so fucking selfish! Think of someone else for a change. Think of Juby, who could be dead in days, hours, minutes even. It occurred to her then, out of nowhere really, that she owed him a great debt. A debt like no other. If he hadn't introduced Inger and Edwin all those years ago her mother wouldn't have been born, and if her mother hadn't been born she wouldn't have been either, which meant that her entire existence on this planet was down to Juby Bench. She had him to thank for her very life, and now *his* life was about to end, and she could do nothing for him except hang about in case he came back in a bad way and needed someone there. It wasn't much, wasn't nearly enough, but what else could she do?

So, for hour after hour Midge sat at her window, taking only short essential breaks for fear of missing his return. A long day, long vigil, some of which she passed polishing Lisette Rainey's chess set, moving it over to the window to work on. One by one the pieces came up gleaming, and when she'd finished, the whole thing looked a treat, its perfection marred only by the absence of the rook in Juby's pocket.

Her grandparents hardly saw her all day, but they didn't intrude or badger her. Edwin fussed a little, privately, worried that something was wrong, but Inger, remembering the oft-thwarted need for privacy in her own childhood, was rather more laid back. 'She's a young woman. Must be sick to the back teeth of us oldies breathing down her neck. Leave her be, Edwin, leave her.'

They couldn't leave her when it was time to go to Jilly Barstow's barbecue, however. When Midge was forced to abandon her post at around 7.50, Juby still hadn't returned.

All day, while Midge sat at her window, reading, polishing the chess set, gazing vacantly, Juby's battered old car had stood in Rouklye's sweltering car park. All day, as usual, he had strolled here and there, but never far from the village now, never again up steep hills or as far as Crowbarrow. When the hour came for visitors to leave, some time after Midge and her grandparents set out for the barbecue, he folded himself back into his car and drove away, not disappointed to be alive still, but nervous about leaving. Another long night beyond the barriers. If it happened out there, all this would have been in vain.

He was about a mile short of Underthorpe when it hit him. A pain such as he'd never known, like a bolt of lightning juddering through him, every part of him. The car swerved, would have slammed into a tree had he not yanked the wheel back just in time – 'Not yet, you don't, not yet!' – and continued on without a pause. He hadn't come this far to be snatched away before he was ready and in the right place, but he knew that he'd just received his final notice. There was no time to waste. He had to get back to Rouklye and stay there till it was over. But first...

Thankfully, the lobby of The Ferryman was deserted, there was no one at the desk, and he was able to get upstairs without being seen. In his room, he boiled the kettle for a flask of tea and packed a small bag with a few provisions. He had no intention of dying of hunger or thirst, whatever else. Then he changed his clothes, thinking, Well I brought these things, ought to put 'em to use this once. Finally he pocketed the wire cutters he'd forgotten earlier and slipped back out to the car.

A quarter of a mile short of the now-guarded sentry post at the head of the Rouklye road, Juby drove onto a stretch of rarely-used track by an overgrown set-aside field. He got out of the car, gave it a little pat like a faithful pet, then, keeping to cover where possible, set off along a secret way of old which had changed hardly at all over the years. And as the light began to withdraw from this humid August evening, Juby Bench entered Rouklye for the last time, alive.

22

All three had been dreading the Barstows' barbecue, if for very different reasons. Edwin dreaded it because he hated large gatherings of people he didn't know, at which he always seemed to spend an eternity listening to the excruciatingly dull life-story or offensive opinions of someone he would prefer not to waste a minute on. Inger dreaded it because Edwin got all sniffy when she drank too much, which she intended to do the moment she heard 'You're not English, are you?', which would require her to explain her origins for the ten thousandth time. Midge dreaded it because, apart from not being in a barbecue mood, she expected to be the only non-adult there apart from Henrietta and Nathaniel. Henry was all right, but the prospect of hanging out with her spoilt brother horrified her.

Dread the evening as they might, the three of them stood all-too-soon before a sign –

TO THE BARBIE!

– that told them this was it and they'd damn well better grit their teeth and get to it. The sign stood at the head of the Barstows' drive, from where they followed a succession of enormous pointing fingers (cardboard) round the side of the house.

It wouldn't be properly dark for a while yet, but in the substantial back garden of the Barstow residence little colored bulbs already glowed in the bushes and trees near the house. A pall of smoke fanned out from the barbecue, which was tended by Wystan himself, in Hawaiian shirt and white cotton trousers. One of the innocuous country music tapes he kept for gatherings of this kind eased the strained pauses of just-introduced guests, most of whom congregated around the patio. There were a few people Inger and Edwin knew – Underthorpers – but most were either out-of-village friends of their hosts or Army colleagues of Wystan's, several of whom had come in uniform in spite of the informality of the occasion.

'Ooh, fancy dress,' Edwin said, far too loudly.

'Behave,' Inger hissed.

Jilly swept toward them, greeted them with a lot more gush than usual, kissing Inger and Midge on each cheek, Edwin on just one because he shrank from Kiss 2, nostrils flaring at the overpowering musk of her perfume. Nearby, a broad middle-aged man in Army uniform stood at the heart of a small attentive gathering, talking in the fruity overloud tones of one who assumes everyone will be fascinated by what he has to say. He had short gray hair and a short gray moustache, and Edwin was much amused by him. 'Didn't think they still made 'em like that,' he muttered.

'That's Colonel Legat,' Jilly said. 'MoD Conservation Officer down from HQ on a visit. Would you like me to introduce you?'

'No,' Edwin replied. 'I'd like you to introduce me to the beer tent.'

Jilly linked arms with him and Inger and walked them away, either completely forgetting about Midge or assuming she would follow. 'The food'll be a while,' she said as they went. 'Wystan had a spot of trouble lighting the coals, but oh, doesn't it smell *wonderful*.'

'Wonderful,' muttered Inger, who had little taste for animal flesh marinated in sweet sauces, then scorched over hot coals. 'Midge!' she called back as they were marched away. Midge moved to follow, but a group of guests to her left suddenly broke up and by the time she got past them her grandparents were just two more heads bobbing round the drinks table – and she was standing face to face with Nathaniel Barstow.

'It's you,' grunted the Brat with little enthusiasm.

'And you,' Midge replied with even less.

This evening Nathaniel was dressed not in camouflage but, at his father's insistence, in pressed jeans, neat shirt, polished shoes. He'd managed to smuggle out an authentic-looking pistol, though, and this he raised between them.

'Password!'

'Oh, gimme a *break*,' Midge said, stepping round him.

The chat was livening up, laughter increasing, as guests relaxed. There wasn't much worth listening to, but when the word 'Rouklye' reached her ears Midge sought the source, which turned out to be the visiting Conservation Officer. She strained to isolate what the man was saying from the rising hubbub.

'... affection for the old place... down here whenever I... servation really got going in the eighties...'

She moved closer, picked up a little more.

'... was a time in the early days when our lads took their targets where they found them... anything that didn't move, and probably a few things that... fair to say we've come on a bit since my department was – '

Heavy rock music at full volume suddenly swamped everything. Heads swiveled to the open patio doors, while

Wystan dropped his cooking utensils and set off for the house waving apologetic hands and grinning wildly to play down the technical hitch. The music went on for about fifteen seconds, ending as abruptly as it had started, replaced by the indignant shouts of the thwarted Nathaniel. Uneasy chuckles from various quarters, conversations cranking up again, Colonel Legat resuming his monologue.

'... pet scheme of this retired sapper, explosives expert, wanted to create a series of pools for dragonflies. Well, when he'd finished there were these damn great holes all over the shop, but I'll tell you something, the man knew his stuff. Nowadays you can't move out there for the – '

Midge wandered off. About to pass the patio doors, she heard Wystan trying to reason with his errant son inside, urgently and quietly, but not so quietly that she couldn't hear every word as she paused to examine a convenient hanging basket.

'Let me down, Nat, and I'll never forgive you. There are some important people here tonight and that sort of behavior does me no good at all. Look, tell you what, be good this evening and we'll take a run into Dorchester next weekend for the record market. What do you say? Just don't show me up tonight, that's all I ask. Deal?'

The Brat must have agreed – silently – for nothing more was said, and shortly afterwards the music started again, not the Iron Maiden that he'd switched to out of devilment, but a muted rhythm-and-blues that was easily talked over. Father and son came out onto the patio and headed for the barbecue, and Midge slipped back into the crowd. Spotting Henrietta across the garden, sitting on a bench with a middle-aged couple, she waved. Henry waved back, looked as if she would like to come over but couldn't because of the company. Midge cruised, hoping to find her grandparents, who were no longer by the drinks. At one point, finding her way obstructed, she stepped sideways without looking and – 'Whoops, steady there!' – collided with the Conservation Officer. The impact caused the colonel's arm to jerk up and whisky to slop over his hitherto impeccable uniform. A large spotted handkerchief appeared in his hand and he dabbed fretfully at his jacket.

'Dear, dear, dear. Dear-oh, dear-oh, dear.'

'Sorry,' Midge said. 'Sorry, I really am.'

He stopped dabbing and smiled, his bristly moustache turning up at the ends, and she realized that his audience had disbanded, possibly with relief, and that she was his new focus of attention.

'Think nothing of it,' the colonel said. 'Accident. Silly place to stand anyway. Guest or resident?'

'Pardon me?'

'Were you invited or are you another of the major's... offspring?'

She shuddered at the second option. 'Invited,' she answered coolly, deciding, since her apology had been accepted, that she wasn't all that keen on chatting to men who approved of blowing holes in Juby's valley, even if it was to encourage dragonflies. She would have moved away, but –

'Local, are you?'

'What?'

'Are you from round here?'

'No.'

'Me neither. Hampshire man originally, currently based in Surrey.'

For Midge it had been a long and gloomy day in which she'd thought of little but Juby Bench and that he was going to die soon, in Rouklye if he could manage it. It seemed likely that if the authorities got wind of his plan they would do everything they could to foil it. The authorities. She looked at Colonel Legat; his whisky-stained uniform, his brisk moustache, his small, twinkling eyes. He looked about fifty, which meant that he wasn't even born at the time of the evacuation, but here, now, in that uniform, he represented the force that had snatched Juby's home from him and soured his life when he was the age that she was now. Juby wasn't the only one who'd lost out in that government-sanctioned theft, of course, and it was this, her personal loss, unsuspected until a couple of days ago – all those unknown, dispersed Millers – that caused a great anger to well up in her, flap in her chest like a trapped bird, and burst out of her mouth in a blind, full-blown fury.

'Just who do you think you are?' she demanded, far too loudly. 'What right have you got to even *be* here?!'

The amiable colonel reeled as though accused of lewd behavior. 'I... I was invited.'

'Not by *them*, you weren't! *They* didn't invite you! You just barged in and kicked them out, and now some of them don't even know their own relatives! Wouldn't know each other if they passed in the street, and all because of you and your... your... '

She simultaneously ran out of steam and realized that all other conversation had stopped and that every eye was on her. She clapped a hand over her mouth, but too late, the damage was done. Inger and Edwin, approaching the scene as her tirade petered out, were among the few who did not look either shocked or amused by what most took for another spoilt kid having a tantrum.

'You know,' Inger murmured, 'I think our Midge is coming out of her shell at last.'

'Where's she off to?' Edwin wondered.

Inger shrugged. 'I'm guessing home.'

'Well, she can't get in without a key.'

'No...'

'Great, the perfect excuse,' and he went after her.

Inger lingered, but just long enough to make their apologies, hers and Edwin's, for leaving early. No apology for Midge, who she was suddenly rather proud of.

23

Before going to sleep the night of the barbecue, Midge had vowed never to show her face in public again. Unfortunately for her, by the afternoon of the following day more people than she'd ever met in her life were clamoring to see it. It all started with an email from her mother.

> Dear all, whatever you hear on the news don't worry, Dave isn't hurt, just held captive. They boarded us in the night, the sneaky sods. Will keep you posted if poss, love Kristin.

'Keep us *posted*?!' Inger shrieked, reading this. 'If *poss*?'

There being no response to her bungled email demands for the whole story, Edwin was dispatched to the newsagent's along the street. While he was gone, Inger and Midge stared wanly at one another, all sorts of appalling thoughts scrambling through their minds. Twice in the past Midge's parents, on other missions, had been arrested and put in jail for a day or two. Once, her father had been beaten up rather badly by some Algerian soldiers for interfering in their business, but they dismissed such consequences as 'par for the course'. Par for the course! In parts of the world, innocent people were losing their heads – literally – merely for being there. She didn't want to *think* what might happen if the Inanians decided to make an example of her non-innocent parents. And it wasn't just them. She knew it was selfish, but if her mother and father were killed what would happen to her?

When Edwin came back laden with the day's papers, Inger swept everything off the kitchen table and spread them out. Three pairs of eyes rapidly scanned page after page but found nothing about the imprisonment of *Earthsave International* activists.

'Kris said their boat was boarded in the night,' Edwin said as they were finishing their search. 'These papers would have been printed before that.'

Inger's eyes widened. 'Why didn't you think of that before we started looking through them? Before you went to *buy* them?'

'Why didn't you?' he countered.

She grabbed the papers, threw them on the floor, and jumped on them.

'What about the radio?' Midge suggested.

'You want her to jump on that too?' said Edwin.

'I mean the news.'

'It's forty minutes to the next news.'

'No, I mean ring them to see if they know anything.'

'Good idea,' said Inger. 'What's the number of the local radio station?'

'How would we know?' Edwin said. 'Anyway, it's not a local event.'

'They have news services, don't they? News could be

coming in even as we sit here twiddling our fingers.'

'Thumbs,' said Edwin.

Inger rushed to the phone, dialed Enquiries rather than waste time looking through the Yellow Pages, scribbled the number she was given, and rang it.

'News desk!' she snapped at the receiver when a voice answered. Then: 'What? No, I don't want a special offer, I want to speak to somebody on the... What are you talking about, I don't have any pets... You're a what? A *vet*? What are you doing being a vet, you're supposed to be a radio station... You're not a radio sta...? Oh, *really!*' She slammed the receiver down and glared at it.

'Try this one,' Edwin said.

He had opened the phone book the moment her confusion started. She looked from the number he showed her to the one she'd written, reversing two digits in her haste – 'Tuh!' – and redialed.

This time she got through, only to be told that no news had come in about captured *Earthsave* people. Was she sure it wasn't a hoax? Again she slammed the phone down.

'You'll break that,' Edwin said.

She glared at him, frustrated and angry. 'Who else can we try?'

'The local newspaper people might have something by now,' Midge offered.

'They might,' Inger said. 'But I think we'll try one of the nationals.' She snapped her fingers impatiently. 'Number, someone, number, number!'

Edwin picked up one of the papers from the floor. 'Where do I look?'

'Wherever you look, Edwin, look in a different one. All they know about on that rag is tits and bums. We don't want to know about tits and bums, we want to know about Dave.'

She scooped up *The Independent*, found a contact number, and dialed it. 'Good morning! Kindly put me through to the news editor!'

Connected almost at once, she asked her question, and heard that information had indeed started coming in about the *Earthsave* ship. She demanded to be told everything. There was some resistance to this, but she got her way by saying that one of the captives was her son-in-law. Midge and Edwin stood tensely at her shoulder trying to make out what was said at the other end. They got some of it, but far from all. When Inger replaced the receiver, less violently this time, she spelt it out for them in three simple sentences.

'The Inanians have commandeered the 'Boldly Go' and taken off all the men. There was a bit of a scuffle. Some minor injuries but no fatalities as far as they know.'

'As far as they *know*?' Midge squawked.

'What about the women?' Edwin asked.

'They left the women on board. Don't seem to have harmed them.'

'You know why they left the women, don't you?'

'No, why?'

'They knew the first thing they'd do would be to dispatch messages like confetti telling the world what had happened.'

'You mean they wanted them to tell?' Midge said.

'Of course. You don't think they want their security people tied up with loony busybodies like your parents, do you? No, they want the governments of the countries to which the various shipmates are attached to demand the return of their citizens so they can get on with their tests in peace. I think they'll be delighted to hand them over.'

When they turned the radio on at eleven the bare bones of the story were delivered as a news item. After that, word spread through the area like a bush fire that the owners of the Underthorpe bookshop were relatives of two of the *Earthsave International* people. Even better, they had the couple's daughter staying with them. Folk came to goggle, in droves.

'They'll be wanting our autographs next,' Inger growled.

'They're welcome to mine,' said Edwin. 'I always fancied a spot of celebrity.'

He would also have rather liked to be on television but when a TV crew turned up to interview them without prior arrangement Inger demanded to know what right they thought they had, barging in on them at such a time. 'It's news,' the would-be interviewer informed her, and asked if he could film them sitting on the couch flipping wistfully through a photo album. Inger suggested that he depart while he and his crew still had all their limbs.

By early afternoon the bookshop was more crowded than it had ever been, mainly with summer visitors popping in for a sight of the relatives of an imprisoned *Earthsaver* and his wife. A few bought books as mementoes, but in the end Inger got so fed up with the constant intrusions that she shooed everyone out, locked the door, and flipped the 'Closed' sign in the faces of those still keen to gawp.

The news didn't change much throughout the day except that the government was reported to be making representations to the Inanians for the release of the four British men, as other governments petitioned for their men. Inger stalked from room to room and up and down stairs, growling under her breath in Norwegian. At one point she spoke it out loud, with some vehemence: 'De jævlene. Jeg håper de råtner i helvete!' ·

'You'd think he was your son, the way you're behaving,' Edwin said to her.

Mistake. She whirled on him.

'Oh, silly me. I was forgetting. No relation at all. Thanks for reminding me, Rainey, now I can relax while they murder my granddaughter's father.'

'*Murder?*' Midge cried.

Edwin clutched his head wearily.

It wasn't until well after a snatched evening meal of bread and cheese that good news came through on the TV

· Translation: 'Those bastards. I hope they rot in hell!'

183

that Inger had commanded Edwin (horrified to learn that the game was up) to bring in from his Pottering Shed. The prisoners had been released on the understanding that their governments keep them away from the test area. Inger and Midge howled with relief and ran at one another; danced about like mad things, whooping for joy. Edwin, not given to such displays unless in the guise of someone else, stood watching with a grin.

Only when she'd calmed down did Midge remember something. Someone. Almost the entire village had popped in during the day, or tried to, plus half the holidaymakers in the region. Everyone but Juby. Juby would surely have come if he'd heard the news. *If* he'd heard. But if he hadn't...

24

Pushing open the door of The Ferryman, Midge saw that the receptionist was the same woman who had directed her to the Breakfast Room on her previous visit.

'I was wondering if Mr. Bench was in,' she said when help was offered, hoping that she sounded more casual than she felt.

'Mr. Bench?' The receptionist peered over her half-glasses. 'Oh, you were here the other day, you're his... granddaughter?'

'No, but he's a friend of my grandparents across the road.'

'Across the road? Not where...?'

She managed to nod and shake her head at one and the same time in an effort to forestall further enquiry. 'Is he in please?'

The woman glanced at the board of hooks behind the desk. 'His key's not here, so he could be. I'll see.'

She tapped out Juby's room number on one of the desk phones and put the receiver to her ear.

A voice behind her: 'Hello! Miss Miller, isn't it?'

Mr. Rackham, bustling out of the TV lounge where he'd been fluffing up cushions for the comfort of guests who might wish to use it.

'Yes,' Miss Miller replied. 'Hello.'

'She's looking for Mr. Bench,' the receptionist informed him. 'I'm buzzing him but there's no answer.'

Midge's heart sank. Juby could have been in Rouklye for the best part of two days and a night, dying, and she hadn't given him a thought since yesterday evening. Some friend.

'Were you supposed to meet him here?' Mr. Rackham asked.

'No, I just thought he...'

She raised her hands from her sides, a small gesture of helplessness that Mr. Rackham responded to.

'What say we go take a peek, to put our minds at rest?'

He reached over the desk for the ring of house keys and

led the way upstairs. Midge followed with some trepidation. Suppose Juby had come back sometime during the day and was up there still, in bed or on the floor – dead?

About half-way along the first landing Mr. Rackham knocked on the door of room 11; waited briefly, knocked again, put an ear to the wood.

'Juby, you there?'

No reply, no sound. He inserted a key in the lock. Midge held back, not wanting to be the first to see. Mr. Rackham opened the door a crack, called once more, wary of bursting in on a guest who might not wish to be disturbed. Still no reply. He opened the door further, put his head round, went in.

'He's not here,' she heard almost at once from outside.

She slipped round the half-open door, into a small room with nondescript blue and gray wallpaper, blue washbasin, over-large walnut wardrobe. A tidy room in which there was nothing of Juby. No sense of him at all apart from the brown suitcase standing at the foot of the bed. Only a case of Juby's could be so old and worn and leathery.

Mr. Rackham tugged the wardrobe doors open. The wardrobe was empty but for a tangled row of hangers. He glanced at the suitcase. 'Looks like he's all packed and ready for the off. Short visit this year maybe. Thought he'd stay at least to the end of the week since he paid till then – in advance. His idea, not mine.'

'Did he sleep here last night?' Midge asked.

'Well of course. He must have.'

'Why must have?'

'Well, because...' He considered, became unsure, then said: 'I'll ask.'

Minutes later, entering by the back door, Midge found Inger and Edwin in the kitchen. They were sitting across from one another, an elbow apiece on the table, right hands clasped diagonally as if about to engage in an arm-wrestle. A bottle and two glasses stood within reach. They were surprised to see her.

'We thought you were up in your room.'

She shook her head. 'I've been over to The Ferryman.'

Inger dropped Edwin's hand. 'The Ferryman?'

Edwin sighed; reached for his glass.

Midge closed the door, leant back on it, hands behind her. 'I went to see if Juby was there. He wasn't. Hasn't been seen since... I don't know.'

'Well that's Juby,' Inger said. 'Slips in and out as the mood takes him, always has.'

'His bed wasn't slept in last night.'

'It wasn't?'

'No, Mister whatever his name is checked.'

'Well, where is he then?'

'I think he's in Rouklye.'

'Rouklye? No, can't be, they'll have shut the gates by now.'

'It's not dusk yet,' Edwin said.

'Not dusk?' said Inger.

'That's when they tell people to shove off. It's still light yet.'

Midge pushed herself away from the door and sat down at the end of the table so that she could look from one to the other of them. 'Something you need to know,' she said.

And she told them. About Juby's visit to the doctor, about his being given six months to live and surviving into a seventh, about his swearing her to secrecy and how wretched she felt breaking her promise. The news shook them, both of them, but, characteristically, it was Inger who was the first to think of doing something.

'Wystan?' she said to Edwin.

He puffed out his cheeks; briefly thought it over; nodded. 'A quiet word in his ear rather than a general alert with klaxons and floodlights,' he said. 'The shock of all that might kill the old boy. That is if he isn't already...'

He glanced at Midge. She was deathly pale.

25

It was admiration for his grandfather's uniform that had lured James Wystan Barstow into the Army as a young man, though his posting to this area nine years ago had not been one that he'd sought. However, he'd settled in easily enough, quietly proud to be following in the footsteps of Major-General Harry Miller, whose name had been on the order to evacuate the Rouklye Valley fifty-six years ago. The downside of the posting was that it entailed so little action that when something like this came up he was more grateful than he cared to let on. Within a minute of Inger's phone call he was on the line to his commanding officer, and once he'd gained permission to proceed changed back into the uniform Jilly had hung up for him less than an hour before. Overhearing his parents talking about some of this, Nathaniel begged to accompany his father, creating such a fuss when refused that he was sent to his personal war room to rail in fury.

The last of the day's visitors had gone by the time Wystan and his three civilian passengers drove into Rouklye. Half a dozen soldiers and two range wardens were waiting by the pond. Wystan told the men to search the village, which they did, quickly and efficiently, reporting back that there was no one in the buildings and sundry accessible parts. He then ordered them to split up and scour other sectors and zones within a couple of miles' radius, reminding them as they set off that they were looking for an elderly gentleman who might be in a bad way, and that they were to treat him with the utmost care and courtesy.

In uniform, Wystan Barstow was a very different individual from the cordial Underthorpe resident who liked rhythm-and-blues, Hawaiian shirts and barbecues. His back was straighter, his shoulders squarer, and he looked as if a smile would be painful as he leant toward Midge and said: 'I just hope this isn't a wild goose chase, young lady.'

For Midge it had been a day like no other. First her father captured by a foreign power, which might have done anything to him, anything at all; then the realization that Juby might have died while her thoughts were elsewhere; then the soldiers' fruitless search of the village; now this, the Brat's suddenly officious father daring her to have brought him here on a fool's errand. She dropped her eyes, near to tears.

Inger tapped the uniform on the shoulder.

'Wystan,' she said. 'In case you missed it, we've been under something of a strain today. We would like nothing better than to put our feet up and shut the world out. We're neither here for the views or trying to waste your oh-so valuable time.'

The major flinched. He'd never doubted that Inger Bjølstad could be a formidable woman when crossed. They'd never had a real falling out in all the years of their acquaintance, but he wasn't sure it was worth testing their fragile friendship with something like this.

'No, I realize that, I'm simply saying – '

'Simply say nothing,' Inger said sharply. 'If Juby isn't here don't even *think* of blaming Midge. She needn't have said a word to anyone, and what if one of your precious day-visitors found his corpse tomorrow? What would the media make of *that*, I wonder?'

While Wystan huffed and shuffled his feet, Midge drifted over to Edwin, leaning on the wall by the row of derelict cottages.

'Not much like a film set now,' he said as she joined him.

'Was that the last time you were here?' she asked. 'When they were making that film?'

'Yeh.'

'Must seem quite strange then. As it is now, I mean.'

'Strange isn't the word. Makes me want to weep.'

'I thought you didn't care about the place.'

He said nothing to this; then, more to himself than to her, murmured: 'I wonder where the bugger's got to...'

Equally stumped, she looked along the row, and saw, down by King George's oak, the almost-there boy, looking her way.

'Think they'd mind if I walked about a bit?' she asked.

'Ask the military man,' Edwin said. 'I'm nobody.'

Returning to Wystan and Inger, she repeated her question. Wystan sucked air. 'Tricky. This is MoD property, and the place is closed to the – '

'Oh, Wystan, don't be so *stuffy*!' Inger cut in. 'The girl wants to take a walk in a perfectly safe area. What do you think she's going to do, ruin the ruins?'

Wystan caved, but with one proviso: 'Just the village, mind.'

Doing her utmost to appear casual and unhurried,

Midge strolled alongside the wall like one who has all the time in the world. The almost-there boy remained at the tree until she drew near, whereupon he took to the track past the church, flickering a little, like a light that would soon expire. She followed him. As she passed the schoolhouse the whispers started, rustling unintelligibly, like old leaves nudged by a minor breeze. There was something comforting in the indistinct voices, something companionable that seemed to urge her on. There were also movements at the corner of her eye, the movements of many, but she looked neither to left nor right for fear the almost-there boy would not be ahead of her when she sought him again.

He paused at the point where the track narrowed, briefly turned as if to make sure that she was still following, and started down. She got a move on, not wanting to lose him, but his head dropped rapidly below the level of the ground she trod, and by the time she began her own descent he was gone. She no longer needed a guide, however. He'd shown her the way. Reaching the bottom of the path, she glanced round to make sure that she wasn't observed, and made for the cordon of tall weeds, irritated with herself for not thinking of this before.

As she parted the tangled barrier the whispers stopped. She saw that the barbed-wire within had been cut and folded back, leaving a clear route through. She stepped forward and the weeds closed behind her with a soft swish. From there, at pains to avoid nettles, thorns, the flailing ends of the severed wire, she passed into a realm of true and perfect silence, at the heart of which the ruined house of Juby's youth, overhung with ancient trees, stood gray and forbidding in the uncertain evening light.

She moved toward the forlorn shell, dreading what she might find inside it.

26

He sat with his back against the wall, newspaper folded before him, constantly adjusting his specs, which seemed intent on finding some path down his nose. His spine hurt. Hard wall to lean against. Coarse, mostly unplastered, digging in. Beneath him the former floor, just a wall-to-wall concrete slab now, ornamented with last year's leaves and other kinds of debris. Across the room, half in shadow, a dead rat, not yet rotting or torn apart by unfussy predators. Nothing deposited or casually cast by human hands, though. No one had entered this house for decades. Visitors to Rouklye who hoped to see everything were thwarted here and elsewhere by tall grasses and weeds, tangled thistles and brambles, barbed wire, notices warning against attempting entry.

He sighed and returned his gaze to the local rag in his hands. He'd looked through it, pausing here and there because that's what you do when you hold a newspaper: turn the pages, fold them, scan the columns, make a show of interest even if you have none. This was all there was now. A local paper, a dead rat, the old wall and floor digging into his back and arse while the day's light faded. The worst of it was that he'd drunk all the tea in his flask. Thirsty but nothing he could do about it. Twice he'd tried to get up and sunk back down, into the same uncomfortable position. For minutes on end, hours maybe, time had ceased to have meaning as he sat there on the rubble-strewn floor, reading or rereading material that held no interest for him, head tilted back, gazing at the darkening blue rectangle above. In the failing light his mind wandered and every so often it seemed as if the sky were a ceiling, and this a room furnished with fat armchairs, a sofa, bulky old sideboard. There was a red and gray floral carpet with a foot-wide gap all round, and chintzy curtains at the windows, and he was a lad again. Over by the fire his bath was waiting, a large tin tub with handles at either end. He saw himself slip off his dressing gown and step in, preposterously tall for his age, sit down quickly to avoid being seen – too quickly, spilling water over the rim. Self-conscious, all ribs and bones and sprouting body hair, he covered himself with the flannel when Mum came in with another pitcher of hot water.

'I dunno what you think you got to hide, Jube, I've seen it all before, y'know.'

Mum? Two contenders for that title. This one, domestic

to the last, brittle and energetic; the other, geologist by profession, frustrated traveler forced to stay home because she had a kid, paying a neighbor to come in and cook, do the washing and ironing. No man about the place, no dad, never had been. Hang on, though. No dad? Course there was. He lived with the sharp-tongued mother. Like her he was very lean, tall, and he had a disapproving mouth, wore a flat cap to work.

Weights pressed down on Juby's eyelids and he was glad to let them close. Easier to see with your eyes shut. See what you want – and remember – block out what you don't.

He was upstairs now, under the blanket. Thick gray bedsocks, hand-knitted. The stone hot water bottle was cold, no comfort at all. Birds starting. He eased himself out of bed, took the blanket with him. The window. Cold early morn, ghost of a tree just yards away. Mrs. Palmer had let herself in the back door. He could hear her downstairs, raking out the kitchen grate. He put his face to the glass to watch her slip out in her crocheted shawl and cast yesterday's ashes across the frosty earth beside the vegetable patch. Back inside now, where she would kneel on the knobbly old hearthrug twisting paper round kindling, light it with a wooden spill, wait till it caught.

He shifted his rump. Uncarpeted floor, hard, rough. He forced his eyes open, tilted his head. No ceiling, no wallpapered rooms to wander through at will, no family. Stop kidding yourself, man. Sort your head out. Records should be set straight at the end.

The end.

Air-raid sirens. Horrendous wailing filling the world. Explosions, distant and not so, glass smashing, running feet, shouts of panic – inside as well as out.

'Under the table, Bets! Come on now! You too, boy!'

Head-first into russet chenille, three tall people jostling for shares of the limited space, Dad thrashing about, angry as ever. 'Agh, there's not enough room, specially with longshanks here!'

'I'll get out then.'

'You stay put, lad.' Dad backed out, stood up, knees creaking. 'I'll sit it out, out here, they'll be done soon.'

'Hubert! Come back, we'll make room!'

Dad flopped into his personal armchair. 'They'll not get me cowering like a whipped dog. Just let 'em try and hit Hubert Bench's house!'

'Oh, don't be so daft! Who do you think's impressed?'

Mum leapt out, ran across the room, seized her husband by the arm to haul him out of his chair and back under the –

Whoom! Crash!

House next door blown apart, taking bits of neighboring houses with it. Bits of theirs.

Peering out through folds of heavy tablecloth, he saw his father half out of the chair, tugged by his lean mother, as the ceiling sagged, opened, disgorged the room above. His bedroom. They didn't make a sound as it came down, and when the dust settled there wasn't a trace of them. Just a big heap of unmoving debris with his bed on top.

'J... Juby?'

The sirens went away. The crashes and bangs, the cries from the street. Someone had come in. Was coming over. Squatting down before him.

'I wondered where you'd got to,' Midge said.

'Uh?' he said.

'You all right?'

He pulled himself together as well as he could.

'All right? Me? Never better.'

His little round glasses had slipped down to the tip of his nose. Setting aside the newspaper, he folded them onto it and smiled a smile that didn't quite work somehow. She was alarmed by the look of him. Alarmed, too, by the house itself, whose forlorn furnishings – an ancient couch with an unnatural dent at one end, a battered dining table, some wonky chairs – looked as if they'd rather be anywhere than here. The scene was very ably completed by jagged shards of broken glass, rubble, weeds, thistles, last year's brittle leaves, something small and dead over there in the corner.

The wall Juby sat against was very rough, its original brickwork mostly exposed, though here and there islands of ancient plaster still clung, one such just to the side of him, half a yard up, host to ribald limericks, salacious wishes, a curiously-shaped vagina, an ejaculating cock, a hangman's noose with a man dangling from it by the neck, and a name,

'William B', the 'William' clear enough but only the top half of the 'B', as if the person engraving it in the plaster had been interrupted before he could finish. *So we meet again, Billy Brooker*, Midge thought. Billy leaving his mark. One of the last things he did, she supposed.

Last things.

She returned her attention to Juby. He wasn't looking at her now, but up, at where a ceiling would once have been. She followed his example, to a small brick fireplace set high in the wall, at the point where the upper floor no longer was. Above that, nothing but sky, darker than it appeared outside, a canopy between ragged verticals. And stars, just a few as yet, and a planet or two she supposed, random pinheads in the taut fabric of gathering night, one of the pinheads moving across and across, as if looking for somewhere to fall or land. Juby saw this too.

'You get a lot of shooting stars in August, here,' he said.

'Yeah?'

'Known for 'em, August at Rouklye.'

She got up from her crouch and went to sit next to him on the rubbled floor. With coarse lumps of debris sticking into her, she re-settled herself until she felt as comfortable as she could, and, like him, leant back against the wall. She felt his sleeve brush her arm. The pale sleeve of a linen jacket she'd not seen him in before. He was even wearing a tie. And he'd shaved. First time she'd seen him totally clean-shaven. It was as if he wanted to look his best at the last.

'Feel a bit wobbly, Evy.'

'You want me to call someone?'

He turned his head. His eyes were sharp. Piercing in the gloom.

'Is there someone with you? I told you to keep it to yourself.'

If he'd had all his wits about him he would have known that she couldn't have come here alone all the way from Underthorpe. But she frowned. Tried to sound offended.

'I said I would, didn't I?'

Satisfied, he sank further into his best summer jacket, which looked even bigger than the black one now. He seemed to be shrinking before her eyes. They sat in silence after this, she hoping against hope that no one would call her name, hoping too that he wouldn't die while she was with him; that they would both get up soon and leave this ruined place, go back to Underthorpe together, somehow.

'Tell Edwin,' Juby said after a while, his voice a feeble rasp that she had to strain to hear.

'Tell him what?'

'Tell him... Nah, no point. But Inger.' He cracked a smile. 'Tell Inger...'

'What shall I tell Inger?'

'Tell Inger that I always...'

Again he didn't finish. Instead he sighed, and said, very quietly: 'Det är väldigt bra att ha varit en man.'

'Come again?' Midge asked gently.

This time no answer at all, and as the last light of day and evening went out of his eyes, they closed, very slowly, quite undramatically.

'Juby?'

Nothing.

Only then did she realize that he'd taken her hand. His enormous hand lightly enclosed hers.

She remained there, unmoving, till the sky closed over their heads leaving nothing but blackness and stars, and she could no longer ignore the voices shouting for her, coming closer, closer. Disentangling her hand from Juby's, she found something in his. Examined it in the final wink of light. His talisman. The fourth rook.·

27

There'd been many written messages, from various sources, mostly supportive, but in two cases of the 'Serve them right, they shouldn't be there' variety. One well-wishing postcard was signed 'Cousin Hector Moorhens'.

'Cousin Hector Moorhens?' Inger asked Edwin.

'Hector Rainey,' he replied. 'Haven't had word from him

· Juby's last words ('Det är väldigt bra att ha varit en man') translate as 'It is very good to have been a man'. This is his adaptation, adding a single 'a', of the Olaf Stapledon line 'It is very good to have been man'. See page 143.

for years. Must have heard all about this stuff on the news.'

'And he's a cousin?'

'Yeh. Ten or eleven years younger than me.'

'You've never mentioned him.'

'I probably have, you rarely listen when I speak.'

'And Moorhens?'

'His house. Nice place, right by the river, not far from Huntingdon. I went there once, just the once, must have been seventeen, eighteen. I had other cousins there too then. I used to send stamps to Clovis – the eldest.'

'Stamps?'

'Old postage stamps. World stamps. Clovis collected them, as did I at the time.'

'Clovis,' Inger said. 'Unusual name for an English boy.'

'I suppose. Never thought about it.' He sighed, adding softly, almost inaudibly. 'Poor kid.'

But Inger heard. 'Why poor kid? Did something happen to him?'

'Nothing that I want to talk about,' Edwin said.

'No, come on, you can't leave it at that. Tell me. Us.'

He gave her one of his very rare scowls. 'Leave it, Ing. We have enough to think about just now – right?'*

The *Earthsave* activists, while forced to stay out of Inanian waters had refused to leave the South Pacific. They'd called a press conference to announce that they would

---

* Clovis Rainey's story can be found in *The Rainey Seasons* (8N Publishing).

remain in the vicinity for as long as the tests were in progress, as observers. If nothing else, they reasoned, this would keep the eyes of the world on the area and perhaps limit Inanian activity to some extent. An email from Kristin Miller, arriving the evening of this dénouement, ended with:

> ... but all being well should be back in time to get
> Midge home to continue her studies. Love Kris

'Ooh, I'm so *honored*,' Midge muttered.

She disposed of her parents and the entire South Pacific affair in the opening paragraph of her latest letter to Ness Friedman. In spite of her decision to hold back on additional news so that she would have more to say on her return home, the rest of the three pages dealt in some detail with how she'd led the soldiers to Rouklye to look for Juby; how his young 'ghost' had materialized to show her where he was; how she'd held Juby's hand while he died. But the moment she started reading all this back she felt as though she were betraying him a second time by turning him into a story for a friend's entertainment, and tore the letter up. This done, she sat cross-legged on the floor looking through the others she'd not yet posted, and found that so much of what she'd written made her squirm now. In the first letter there were dismissive comments about Underthorpe and snarky remarks about the boring old people she was stuck with, and in the others clever-clever asides about the way Juby looked, his nostalgia for the 'old days', his mood-changes, and so on. Disgusted with herself, she tore these up too, and after consigning the pieces to the waste bin set her back against the side of the bed to mull over what Edwin and Inger had told her a couple of hours ago at the kitchen table.

'What do you mean, Juby wasn't from Rouklye?' she'd said when she heard.

'Did he say he was?' Edwin asked. 'I mean actually *say* that?'

'He must have, where else would I have got it from?'

'Well, he wasn't. His mother was. Born there, she was, but when she was a young woman she met Hubert Bench (he was a guard on British Railways, a miserable sod even then) and moved up to the smoke with him. Juby was born in a two-up, two-down in Maida Vale.'

'But all his talk of being a boy in Rouklye...'

'Oh, he was no stranger there,' Edwin said. 'His folks didn't have much time for him, you see. They would put him on a train at the start of the school hols from the age of five or six, and me and Mum would meet him at this end. It started as a one-off visit, I believe, but became a regular thing when he responded so well.'

'He traveled all that way on his own at *five*?' said Inger, to whom this detail was also new.

'Or six, not sure. But yes. Can't imagine young kiddies being packed off like that nowadays, can you? Juby loved staying with us. My mum wasn't a cuddly woman, independent as hell, no time for men, but she was open and amusing, and she liked Juby. Saw something of herself in him, I think. But what most clicked for him about Rouklye was all the space and freedom after being cooped up in London with parents who didn't give a monkey's for him. He used to get in a right state the night before he was due to go home. When Bet and Hubert copped it in the Blitz, Mum took him in. Dream come true for Jube.'

'A dream that didn't last,' Inger said.

'He was beside himself when the eviction notice came,' Edwin said. 'I never saw him so angry. He'd already lost one home and here he was about to lose another. One he was very attached to. He stomped about the valley for days, swearing at the top of his voice. You could hear him effing and blinding a mile away.'

'Where did he go to live when he left Rouklye?' Midge asked.

'With me, initially. My digs. Bed-sit in Wareham. Couple of months, no more. Juby had to sleep on the sofa, which was much too short for him. He wouldn't let it go, what happened to Rouklye. Went on and on about it, drove me barmy. I broke open a fresh bottle of milk the day he moved out.'

'Where did he go next then?'

'Got himself a room over The Greyhound Inn at Corfe. Worked in the bar to pay for it. He wasn't really old enough, but at sixteen he was well over six foot and still growing, so he got away with it.'

'I've been meaning to ask,' Inger said to Midge. 'How did you know where to find him at the end?'

A small shrug. 'He'd been trying to cut his way through to the house for days. It was where he most wanted to be.'

'But why that old place?' This was Edwin.

'It was his home,' she said, surprised that he should wonder. 'He was happy there. Yes, I know,' she added when he frowned, 'it was your house, but he did spend all those holidays there, and he did live there with you after his parents were killed.'

'No, he didn't,' Edwin said.

'Uh? But you said – '

'We didn't live there. No one did in our time. It was always empty, that old place. Boarded up. Wasn't a ruin back then, of course. Still had a roof and a top floor, though the stairs were a bit dodgy. We used to break in, add some artwork to the walls, compete to see who could pee the highest, all the usual laddish shenanigans.'

'Doesn't sound like the Juby I knew,' Inger said.

'Oh, Juby didn't go in for that stuff. Just the village lads.'

'Including you?'

'Naturally. My duty as one of the boys. No, Midge, our house – just a cottage really, semi-detached – was the other direction entirely, up beyond the church. I had a scout round for it when you went off to find Juby. Hardly anything of it now, and easy to miss with all the trees that've grown up around it.'

She was at a complete loss. 'But he called the *other* place his house. He even showed me his bedroom window.'

Edwin frowned at this, plainly mystified, but then said, very slowly: 'Now that I think of it...'

'What?' Midge said.

'He as good as took that old dump over when he moved down in forty-one. It hadn't been lived in for years. Cold as hell, damp too, too near a stream it was said, or built over one. He slept there sometimes, not sure on what, there wasn't a bed there. Mum let him get on with it. She approved of independence. I wasn't like that. Not half as adventurous as either of them. I think the only time she came close to being proud of me was when I left home at fourteen. Showed initiative, you see. Character.'

'But why would he say he *lived* there?' Midge asked.

'It's not so hard to understand,' said Inger. 'A place of his own, furnished from his imagination...'

'Always did have an imagination, old Jube,' Edwin said.

Inger smiled sadly. 'Yes. He did.'

Then, finally, there'd been the bombshell to beat them all. The admission that explained so much and turned Midge's world on its head. It was Edwin who broached the subject. 'Midge' he said. 'In the light of everything, there's something else we feel you should know.'

Inger shot a glare his way. 'You feel, not me.'

'All right, me,' he said.

But it was she who took up the narrative. 'Another antediluvian tale, I'm afraid, and if it were not told I'm sure no one would be any the worse for it, but this fellow has decreed that we must come clean, and I... well, I suppose we do owe it to you.'

'Go on,' Midge said, suddenly nervous.

'You remember my journey with Juby from Amsterdam to England, and his first visit to Rouklye since the war, and how he was so upset by what he found there that he shot off without a word?'

'Yes...'

'Well, he left me pregnant.'

'He what?' Inger just looked at her. 'You mean... my mother wasn't your only child?'

'No, I don't mean that. Kristin was my one and only.'

'Sorry, I don't...'

'She's Juby's daughter,' Edwin said.

'Juby's daugh...' She couldn't finish.

He reached out, touched the back of her hand lightly with a finger. 'You're his granddaughter, Midge. Sad as it makes me to put it into words, you're Juby's blood, not mine.'

She frowned at him. Then shook her head. 'No. You're my grandpa. Everyone knows that.'

'Everyone *thinks* that,' he said, 'including your parents – and believe me I wish it were true – but, well, there you are. It's a wonder, seeing as Inger's always going on about not giving a fig for what people think, that she agreed to my proposal that she stay in Underthorpe and pretend the child was mine, rather than return home and face her family.'

'My father was a strict Methodist minister,' Inger put in. 'If he had learned the truth his outrage would have made my mother's life a misery. She was not a strong woman. The complications of family life, Midge. Take my advice: find a nice cave away from it all and become a hermit.'

It was just too much to absorb all at once, too much rearranging of the past to undertake in minutes. Later, later. 'But Juby knew?' she ventured. 'About the baby?'

Edwin shook his head. 'He wasn't around, we had no idea where he'd gone, and by the time he resurfaced Kris was about to start school, and it seemed too late somehow.'

'But didn't you tell my mother when she was older?'

'Never quite found the moment,' Inger said. 'Do you think she should be told?'

'I don't know. Bit late now, probably.'

'Yes. So what do you say we keep it to ourselves, just the three of us? Our little family secret.'

'*Little?*' Midge said, and sat back, completely drained.

28

Juby's old-fashioned glasses, his little round specs, had

become an ornament of sorts. Part of a display in her room. She'd placed them beside an old hourglass that Inger had no use for, the hours speeding by quickly enough at her age, she said, without being reminded of them by trickling sand. Every couple of days she, Midge, brought a few small flowers in from the garden and added them to the arrangement – not flowers of mourning but of life and color, which she hoped Juby would have approved of.

And the fourth rook. It was back where it belonged. Not in Rouklye, where it hadn't originated anyway, but on the now-gleaming chess board, alongside the hourglass and specs. Feeling that she ought to know a bit about the game after all that had happened, she'd borrowed a *Chess For Dummies* from the shop, from which she learnt that each piece had a function of its own. King, queen, knight, bishop, rook, pawn, they all moved in different ways around the board. The rook's moves – surprisingly, given that Juby had carried one with him for so long – were among the most direct, traveling only in straight lines, horizontally or vertically, until it reached a square occupied by an opponent's piece. As a symbol of Juby's life and character it didn't work. She doubted that he'd ever been much of a one for strict rules or straightforward advancement, though he'd certainly had a single-minded objective at the last.

Not thinking of anything in particular, she picked up the book of poems, *On the Bleak Ridge*, and idly turned some of its pages. She'd asked Edwin if he knew anything of its author and he said that he couldn't recall ever hearing of a William in the family. Well she, Midge, clearly wasn't related to him either, but there was something that she'd read in this collection of his that she suddenly felt an urge to read again. She found it, sat down on the floor, and, as before, read the poem aloud, slowly.

We each took a step backward,
As though quitting a circle
We'd been caught occupying by mistake.

Old identities had no place here.

And in the wink of an eye
They were lost to us, the people we'd known,
The places we'd lived in and visited,

The hopes, the joys, the whole caboodle.

Not a whisper remained of past events,
Of sights or sounds or incidents.
Like lost souls we moved off on the long road.

The stars were very bright.

It hadn't meant anything before, but this time it felt like a description of the parting of the ways of she and Juby in the remains of the house he'd thought of as his, once. It was as if this William Rainey knew her, or Juby; had been there, with them. Or was one of them. One or both.

She was still sitting on the floor, cross-legged, when she got that prickly feeling of not being alone. She glanced to her right, half-expecting to find the almost-there boy waiting to be noticed. But it wasn't the almost-there boy, it was her reflection in the chevalier mirror. She set the book of poems aside and got to her feet. So did Mirror Midge. They advanced on one another, and each spread the fingers of one hand on the glass, the right hand of one, the left of the other; touched fingertips. Each studied the other's face. *Rare birds, you and me, Evy. Rare birds.* Rare as in unusual, she thought. Out of the ordinary. I am an unusual, out-of-the-ordinary person. Not like anyone else, anywhere. Well, just one other. The gawky awkwardness, the ratty hair, the big nose, they made sense now.

'Thanks a lot, Juby Bench.'

She dropped her hand. So did Mirror Midge. But when they stepped away, the real Midge Miller was the one who did not live in a mirror. And as she went out to the landing and started downstairs she knew something else, though it went unvoiced, even unthought in concrete terms: that when she was back home, telling Ness about everything that had happened (editing and highlighting where necessary) it would be she, the Midge who'd stepped back from this side of the mirror, who, just for once, would be the one to envy and point out admiringly to friends.

29

Inger and Edwin had been on the point of arranging a small
service for Juby in Underthorpe church when Midge told
them of his horror of such an event, and his request to be
taken to Rouklye. Inger at once approached the authorities,
but was refused permission to bury him in the churchyard.
No one had been buried there for years and they weren't
about to make an exception for someone who'd lived most of
his life abroad. But they agreed to allow his ashes to be
deposited there at an appointed time, after the day's visitors
had gone.

So it was that just after dusk on a fine August evening
that a sturdy gray urn in a scuffed leather satchel that had
belonged to Edwin's mother was carried – by Edwin himself
– to Rouklye churchyard. Army representatives and soldiers
kept a discreet distance while the small group gathered
around the spot to which Midge directed them; the patch of
grass Juby had claimed for himself with the stamp of a
sandaled foot. Five of the mourners were Juby's family,
who'd come over from Sweden after Inger phoned with the
tidings. Midge hadn't had much to do with the Müellers
since their arrival that afternoon. There'd been so little time,
and besides, conversation was far from easy. Juby's daughter

Johanna, who only vaguely resembled him, spoke excellent English, but her husband's was very limited and the two girls, if they knew any, didn't attempt it. The third child, the boy, having been taught English as a second language all through his school years, was very fluent, though he seemed to want to keep to himself. Midge had difficulty keeping her eyes off Juby Müeller. He was his grandfather to the life, exceptionally tall, with the same bushy hair, but dark brown rather than gray. He even had the same nose, though it wasn't yet as developed as the old man's. Even more disconcerting than his features, however, was that every now and then she caught him staring at her. The stare was that of the almost-there boy.

Edwin asked if he might be the one to scatter the ashes. 'Juby and me,' he said, 'we were close in our day.'

There were no objections.

He emptied the urn very carefully over the chosen spot, in a slow arc so that a heap would not form. Midge found it hard to believe that that long streak of a man could be contained within such a modest vessel. Edwin slapped the pot two or three times to dislodge malingerers, which shot forth, whirled in a hesitant final dance, and expired on the short springy turf with the rest. Midge wondered what was wrong with her. Shouldn't she be more moved by all this, or sadder, or – something? She glanced at the others to see how they were affected. Although Edwin's brow was more furrowed than usual, his expression was otherwise unreadable as he stared at the ashes he'd deposited. Juby's fair-haired granddaughters looked rather bemused by the whole business, but on their mother's cheek there was a single slow tear. Their father stood straight-backed throughout, appropriately solemn, while the boy stood apart from everyone, avoiding all eyes. Only Inger turned away so that her face could not be seen, shoulders shaking silently.

And then an odd sensation came over Midge. Whether it was the mellow evening light or the mood of the occasion she couldn't have said, but she felt a small warm shiver, and suddenly there seemed to be nine of them there – nine where there should be eight. She counted, and eight there were, but the feeling persisted that another now stood among them. She touched Inger's arm.

'Would it be all right if I went down there for a minute?' She gestured in the direction she wanted to go.

'I'll ask.'

Glad of the distraction, Inger hastened to the steps, where a captain leant against the gate waiting for them to finish so his men could soak Juby's ashes into the ground with watering cans. Midge met her half-way as she returned.

'Permission granted, as long as you don't go in this time.'

30

In the few days since Juby's death – perhaps as a result of it – most of the rampant brambles, thistles and other tall weeds this side of the house had been hacked down. The warning signs were still there, more visible than ever, and the repaired wire fence; but for the first time she had a clear view of the ruin from outside. She gazed at it without really focusing, her thoughts not on the house particularly, or anything else she could put a name to, but in no-man's land, no-Juby land, no-Midge land; so adrift in nothingness that when the silence was suddenly punctured by a harsh cry followed by a frantic high flurrying, she returned to the present, and the place, with something like shock. Looking up, she saw a large black bird leap from the dense foliage. Free of the trees, the rook soared, twisted and tumbled through the air, as though performing for her benefit.

I always had this idea that if the rooks came back, if just one returned...

As she thought this she heard another sound, a much smaller sound, and whirled round, stared at the tall figure at the top of the rise. 'You made me jump,' she said.

Young Juby Müeller stammered something in his own language, but quickly corrected himself. 'I wondered where you were going.'

'Why?'

Painfully shy at the best of times, it had taken courage

for the boy to go after her. 'I'm sorry,' he said, and turned to go.

'No, wait,' Midge said. 'It's okay.'

He stopped. 'Are you sure?'

'Yes. Stay.'

Young Juby relaxed a little but did not complete his descent. 'What is that building?' he asked.

'What building?' There was only one in the immediate vicinity, but she needed time to think what to tell him.

'That one, that ruin.'

'It was... your grandfather's house.'

He virtually gaped. 'That's where he *lived*?'

'It's where he died,' she nearly said, but stopped herself just in time; instead said: 'Yes.'

The boy, excited, enthralled, no longer inhibited, almost jumped down the path. 'But it's so *different*,' he said, halting at the bottom, eyes raking the decapitated building.

He was standing beside her, but she had to look up at him. He really was very tall for his age. 'Have you seen an old picture or something?'

'No, I...'

'You what?'

'I dreamed it.' He rushed it out, as if realizing how foolish it sounded.

'You *dreamed* it?' Midge said.

'I dreamed of the whole village. But it wasn't like this. It wasn't fallen. Ruined.'

216

'Tell me about your dream.'

'Not just one,' he said. 'There have been many. They began shortly after Farfar left. I dreamed of walking here and of being in a little school, and of a road to the sea. In one dream I stood on high cliffs and watched a fierce storm.'

'Were there any people in your dreams?'

'I saw only one person,' he replied.

'Your grandfather?'

'No. Not him. I was aware of him, but he was always not quite present. I felt... sensed... a great pain in him. In the final dreams I knew...'

'Knew?'

'What would happen to him.'

Midge took a long breath, then asked who it was that he'd seen in his dreams if not his grandfather. Young Juby looked directly at her but seemed reluctant to answer the question.

'Who?' she repeated.

Then, quietly, almost with embarrassment: 'You.'

'Aaah.'

So there it was. As it had been all the time. The almost-there boy. He hadn't been Juby Bench's younger self, he'd been Juby Müeller dreaming of the Rouklye his grandfather had described in such fond detail. When he walked here in his dreams, this boy had seen not a pitiful huddle of unroofed buildings and fenced-off woods presided over by the military; he'd seen the beloved haven of a storyteller's youth. And he'd encountered just one person. An unmet blood-cousin.

'Did we speak in these dreams of yours?' Midge asked.

Juby Müeller shook his head. 'I tried to speak with you, but no words came, and I couldn't hear you when you seemed to be speaking.' He attempted a wry smile. 'But here you are, in life. No dream. Crazy stuff, huh?'

Crazy. Oh yes. What could be more crazy than your dream-self walking around a place you'd never visited, as it was in its heyday, and being seen by non-dreamers in broad daylight? One non-dreamer anyway. But was it any crazier than ghosts, magic, belief in a supreme being?

She looked again at the house in which Juby Bench had taken his final breath while holding the hand of the granddaughter he didn't know he had.

'You see that window up there?' She pointed. 'That was his bedroom. He told me he used to wake up as it got light and lie there listening to the dawn chorus.'

It wasn't quite what he'd said, but she wanted to give the boy something to carry with him as this sad day receded into his past. Young Juby frowned, not understanding 'dawn chorus', but was then lost again in the remains of the old building that rose up before him.

'When I'm back home in Uppsala,' he murmured, 'I'll see him at that window.'

'Me too, in Winchester,' Midge said. 'Michigan too, if I ever make it back there.'

The rook that had returned to the village cawed sharply once more, as if to rebuke them for ignoring it, then sank back into the trees: the nest it had made.

'Midge! Gotta go!'

Edwin stood at the top of the path.

'Coming,' she said.

He turned and headed back. Midge started up the slope.

'Midge?' Juby Müeller said, following. 'Is that your true name?'

'Why wouldn't it be?'

'I wondered, that's all.'

'My proper name's Evy. But Midge is what I'm called. Usually.'

'I like Evy,' Juby Müeller said. 'Good name.'

She glanced over her shoulder, down at him. Was he making fun of her? The look on his raised face seemed to belie that. She continued her ascent, and as she did so heard a number of voices from beyond the rise. Reaching the top, she saw, in the gentle evening light, men who hadn't been there before leaning on garden walls that also hadn't been there, and women tutting kids, others chatting to neighbors. Houses and cottages had roofs and doors, there were curtains at windows, flowers in gardens, cats on ledges, dogs mooching by gates. Rouklye was whole again, and occupied not by military forces but by ordinary people living the kind of lives that had been lived here for generations. Then came the birdsong, oceans of birdsong, enough to fill all the woods of old Rouklye. A perfectly-staged scene, as flawless as an old man's rose-tinted picture of a bygone age. But it was also, somehow, as though the ruins and the soldiers and the tanks on numbered hillsides were the unreality; that this was the way things should be.

And then it was gone, all of it: the chirrups and whistles of the birds; the cozy chatter of the people; the flowers; the animals; the curtains; the roofs. Silence returned, along with the soulless ruins, deep in weeds, laden with ivy, crouching in the casual shadows of antique boughs.

'Did you see?' she whispered as Juby Müeller joined her at the top of the path. 'Did you *hear*?'

He said nothing, but as they walked together past the schoolhouse to join the others waiting by the King's oak, Midge glanced slyly at him. A faraway look had crept into his pale gray eyes; a look she knew very well indeed.

And there was a trace, she noticed, just a trace, of a smile on his lips.

Evy Cobb: Afterword

Rouklye, twenty-one years later. August again, and again a sizzler. In all these years the world outside has changed in countless ways. Fortunes have been made and lost, self-serving dictators and other scumbags have risen and fallen, well over a billion people have been born, yet the Rouklye Valley is still MoD property, the woods and many other parts are still out of bounds, there are still warning notices at every turn, barbed-wire fences, padlocked gates. No tanks on hillsides, though. Not that I've seen so far. No giant numbers either. Probably just means they're somewhere else today.

We're here because of me. A whim of mine. A wish to revisit Rouklye after all the years back home, where I went to live as soon as my folks could be persuaded to let me be an Actual American again, lose the English accent I'd struggled for years to get right so I wouldn't stand out in crowds. I didn't go back to Michigan, though, but to Cooperstown, NY. I went there because Cooperstown is where Oliver Robert Cobb hails from; Ollie, who I met over here when I'd barely turned twenty, him serving his final USAF posting at one of the bases, and allowed myself to be dragged not too unwillingly to his hometown. I like Cooperstown. I could get by without the baseball obsession but I love the memorabilia shops, the older architecture, the museums, galleries, the Catskills – and we go boating on Otsego Lake a fair bit. Can't imagine living anywhere else now.

Imagine? Well, I can. Course I can. But England? No. England's the past for me. A place to visit for nostalgia's sake, most of the nostalgia being for this old place. My boys will never understand the feeling I have for Rouklye. No reason why they would. Feelings can't be shared, not really, only described, written about, suggested. But this place. It's so deep within me that sometimes, thinking about it, of what happened here, it's hard not to let out a howl of some sort, or at least a muted sob, a sly sigh.

Most of the ruins are as I remember them, but a few previously enclosed by trees and out-of-control weeds have been partially rebuilt and made accessible. I take one of these to be the semi-detached cottage where Edwin grew up and Juby spent his vacations and went to live for a time before the evacuation. A display board with four photographs stands in front of the building. The first print, the only one in black-and-white, shows it as it was in 1943, double-storied, a tiled roof, two small gated gardens, washing on a line in one. In the next photo, dated 2005, all that remains are bits of crumbling lower wall draped with brambles, while in the third, taken two years later, the structure is surrounded by scaffolding, with the walls a bit higher. In the final picture it's as it appears today – still no roof, doors or windows, no hint of a garden, but with the walls rebuilt to a point a little above the first floor. Below the photos there's a printed message.

> These two cottages have been partially renovated for general viewing at a cost of £55,562, which funds have come from voluntary car park donations, church sales and public subscription. Please treat the building with care.
>
> Army in co-operation with the public

I can think of a couple of people who, if they were still about, might see the irony of this. The tenants of a pair of perfectly good cottages were evicted with the approval of a democratically-elected government and their homes used for target practice or allowed to crumble by the new owners, who, years later, are accepting public donations for a token rebuilding scheme to show that their hearts were in the right place all along in spite of the rumors. I can almost hear Edwin's dry chuckle – probably in someone else's tones – and Juby's hoot of derision.

From here I climb the steps to the churchyard. Stand a minute or two by the patch of grass on which we scattered Juby's ashes. 'Hello, old boy,' I say, very quietly. I listen, but nothing comes back. There's no sense of him now. There are no whispers. No almost-there boy.

After this there are just two places I need to see.

Heading back down the steps I see my three men peering into the old telephone kiosk at the far end of Post Office Row. Can't help but smile, the boys being here today. Given their names, I mean. Ollie didn't mind the names. Sadly for them, both Juby and Edwin have inherited 'the nose', but that's one of their few physical likenesses. Twins they might be, but identical they're not. Virtual opposites of their late namesakes too. My Juby might shoot up in a year or two, but at present he's a couple of inches shorter than Edwin, a bit plumper, and his hair is easily controlled. And it's Edwin, whose hair is constantly all over the place, who shows signs of becoming a bit of a tearaway.

Love my lads as I do, I'm not ready to join them yet. I slip across the way into the old schoolhouse. Inside, it's almost exactly as I remember it. The photo of the children who took lessons here in 1912 still hangs in the little cloakroom; and beyond, in the vaulted classroom, oil lamps still dangle from the ceiling. The only person here, I stand a moment, looking, absorbing. It's so utterly silent, so still, as if holding its breath before a batch of kids rushes in, shouting, laughing, shoving. The piano's still here, and the rows of linked desks, the blackboard on its easel beside the fireplace, though with different information and suggestions as to what to look for outside.

Rookeries are mentioned.

Leaving the school, turning left onto the steep track

down to the last building I have to visit, I find that the surrounding woods have been cut back and the barbed-wire removed. The house looks much the same from the outside, but work's been done to make it safe to enter. Anyone can wander into it now. I don't like that much. Doesn't seem right that strangers can stroll round Juby's adopted home. I could go in myself, but if I do I know I'll see him sitting on the rubbled ground in his best clothes, feel his dead hand in mine, and his cherished talisman.

I turn away. But as I turn, I catch a movement in the ragged upper reaches of the building. I squint up through a shaft of rusty sunlight and see a tall figure gazing out from one of the window spaces. I blink, and he's gone, and I decide that the ancient light of Rouklye has played one last trick on me. But as I leave this place forever, never to return, I give that empty window a little wave, in case I didn't imagine him.

Juby Bench. My friend. My grandfather.

Evy Cobb's Family Tree

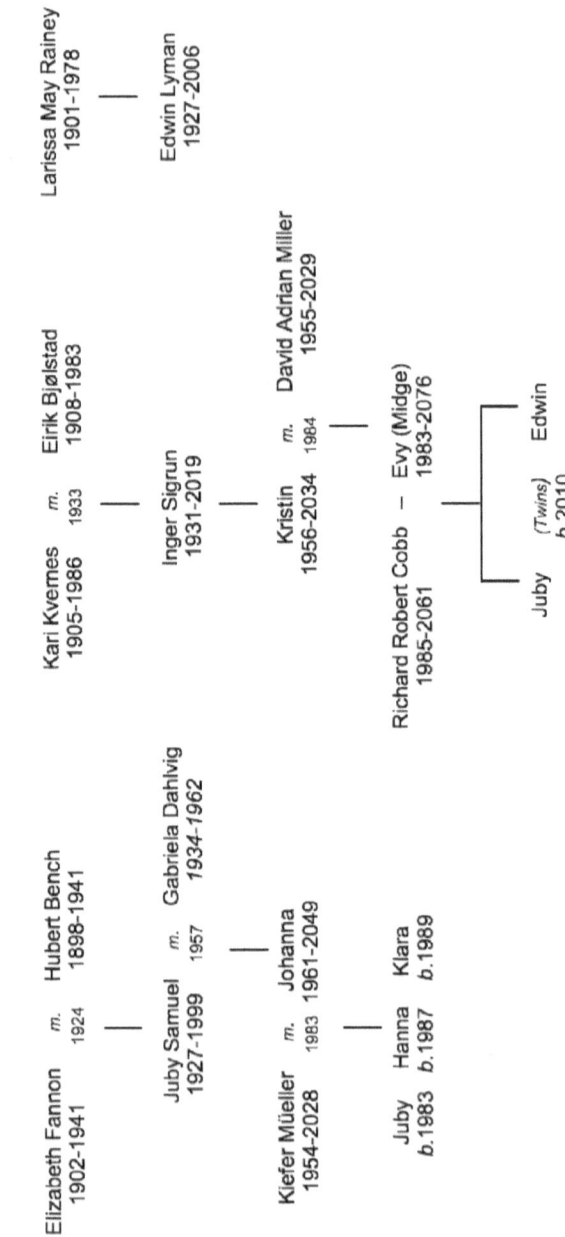

The Rainey Links Sequence
THIS RUINED PLACE
THE RAINEY SEASONS
THE SILENCE OF BLEAKRIDGE

These three books may be read singly or in any order, though if read in the order shown above the reader might be pleased to discover small links and nudges to the other two which could otherwise be missed.

Volume Two, **The Rainey Seasons**, follows two versions of the Rainey family, who, each unknown to the other, live in a riverside house called Moorhens (the house the author was born in). The youngest characters, 20 year old Miriam and Cal, are alternate versions of the same person but of different sexes. They have never met; haven't the faintest inkling of one another's existence. But they *will* meet, and because of that meeting their lives, their entire histories, will change dramatically, without anyone but them being the slightest bit aware of it.

See next page for an extract from
THE RAINEY SEASONS

That extract is followed by discussion questions about
This Ruined Place.

THE RAINEY SEASONS
Prelude

Black October night. Rain hammering the windscreen. Rhythm of the sluggish wipers scrambling my thoughts, returning me to the year everything changed. Changed twice in three short seasons. The first dramatic, emphatic, heartbreaking, the second leading to this, all these years on, running from betrayal with a little passenger inside me. Driving home to preserve a family tradition.

To bring a child into the world at Moorhens.

I've lost the habit of trying to pinpoint critical instants when futures swing in the balance, but tonight, bitter as hell, cursing the dark, the weather, everything, everything, I wonder at what point it went wrong this time. One point or many? All those tangent-filled split-seconds when a life might veer in any direction, any at all. The numerous tiny moments when everything can change – *does* change – and you never know it.

Never suspect it for a minute.

Chapter One / Day Seven
LENA, 41

Two years. Two to the day, and no one's mentioned it. Trying to forget it ever happened perhaps. But I can't forget. The second anniversary of your death isn't something you can easily set aside.

'Starting to snow,' I say.

He shrugs. 'Won't settle.'

'The forecasters beg to differ. And you have a long drive.'

'I'll put my foot down, beat it there.'

'Don't you dare.'

'Get there?'

'Drive like an idiot.'

It was a day like this. Very like it in the beginning, far from like it at the end. A rail, a single rail, weakened by what came to be called a 'rolling contact fatigue crack', made so brittle by the freezing conditions of previous weeks that when the wheels of that particular train on that particular night lumbered across it, it shattered into more than three hundred pieces and the engine jerked upward, taking two of the carriages with it. I was in the second carriage. Several of my fellow passengers died instantly. No seatbelts, so where do you go? Any damn where, that's where, crash-crash, smash-smash. I remember nothing of it, or of the hours that followed. I was one of those whisked off to Addenbrooke's as soon as the ambulances reached us. They operated on me right away apparently. Me and I don't know how many others. Some of the others survived. But me?

I didn't make it.

I was gone. Well and truly gone.

But they brought me back. Against all the odds, they

brought me back. Don't ask me how. All I know is that I died and I've never felt quite right since – in the head, the heart – though the only person I let it show to is the Lena in the mirror, when we're alone. Two years later, as fit and well as can be expected, in body if not mind, I insert one of Joe's arms into his overcoat. He shakes me off.

'I can't drive in this.'

'You'll need it,' I say.

'There's a heater,' he replies.

'It'll take a while to make a difference. You can pull in to a lay-by and strip off when you're warm enough.'

He gives in, but when I start brushing the coat's shoulders, he says, 'Lene, will you for Christ's sake leave me *alone?*'

'You look a mess,' I tell him.

'I'm comfortable as a mess. I swear, if I dropped dead this minute you'd tidy me up before the body-baggers got here.'

'Goes without saying.' I raise my voice. 'Mim, he's off, break open the champagne!'

Miriam emerges from the kitchen nibbling toast. 'Already open.'

Joe says, to both of us as if addressing children: 'Now what's the procedure while I'm away?'

'Procedure?' one of us asks.

'With strangers at the door.'

'Er... don't open it to them?'

'Correct.'

'How will we know if they're strangers unless we open the door?'

'Well, you look through the window *beside* the door, what else?'

'What if they're strangers who want to read the meters?'

'Why would they want to read the meters?'

'Their job maybe?'

'Are the meters due to be read?' he asks me.

I jerk a shoulder. 'But if they *are* meter readers,' I say, 'should we let them in or tell them to take a hike?'

'Depends if they can prove they are.'

'How would they do that?'

'You ask to see their IDs, of course. They have to have IDs if they're legit.'

'Ah,' says Mim, 'but how will we know their IDs are *genuine*?'

At last realizing that he's being set up, Joe says, 'Look, you two. Listen. There's a lot of dodgy characters about these days, and our nearest neighbor is not only too far away to hear your screams, but stone deaf, so stop being a pair of smart-arses and take *care*, all right?' He picks up the canvas holdall he dropped by the door earlier. 'Give you a ring tonight,' he says to me. 'Mid-evening sometime.'

'You'll be there before that.'

'I'll need to settle in.'

'Go out on the town with your bit of stuff, you mean.'

'I'll tell her that's what you call her.'

'She knows.'

He brushes our foreheads with his lips, steps backwards into the porch, and heads for the garage hunched against whirling snowflakes that suddenly seem out to get him. Mim and I wait dutifully in the porch, arms tightly folded, shoulders high, as he pulls the garage doors back and goes inside. Soon, if not soon enough – it's not warm out here – we hear the engine turn over. Then the car backs out, crunching gravel, reverses in a tight semicircle.

'Drive carefully!' I yell, the way you do.

He gives a ha-ha-devil-may-care wave and the stripped trees and bushes that line the drive squeeze out silver flashes all the way to the gate, at which point the oddest feeling comes over me.

'What?' Miriam says.

I glance at her. 'What what?'

'You said "He could be driving out of my life".'

'I said that? Out loud?'

'You did.'

I pull a face. 'My mind needs a padlock.'

'Are you two all right?' she asks.

'All right? Us? Why wouldn't we be?'

'What do I know, I'm just the daughter. He might have shut the garage doors.'

'I'll see to them later.'

'Could be half full of snow by then.'

'Nothing stopping you doing it.'

She shivers. 'Huh!'

'Plans for the day?' I ask, closing the door.

'If I say sweet Fanny Adams will you promise not to do your usual?'

'Fanny Adams,' I say brightly. 'Eight year old girl horribly murdered by a solicitor's clerk in Hampshire, August 1867.'

She rolls her eyes. 'And your dad told you that when you were Fanny's age and it still makes you shudder to think of it, I know, I know, I *know*.'

'Speaking of dads, with yours out from under, we can clean the house, put everything back in order, yippee.'

She groans. 'I should have gone with him. I could have, but no, I chose to stay with the only person in the world who has to have the fridge magnets in perfect alignment.'

I open the first door off the hall. 'I'll do in here, you start on other rooms.'

'I haven't finished my breakfast,' she says.

'Well, when you have... please?'

In the Long Room I open the curtains. The uninspiring view of the south garden from the French windows is already improved by the drifting snow. The snow does something else too. Takes me back to last night. That old familiar feeling that I shouldn't be here. That the two of them should be carrying on without me. From there I got to wondering what the house would be like if I hadn't been clawed back to life without my consent. Would they have looked after it? Kept it tidy? Cleaned, dusted, all the rest? Pathetic stuff. As if such things matter. But in the night such idle maunderings are hard to switch off. Impossible, even.

Well, morning now, and Joe away for a couple of days, and – whisper it – I feel mildly liberated by the thought of not having to include him in my personal equations, accommodate him in all the customary ways. It's different with Mim. I'm never happy when she's out of reach. I owe her everything, always will. I've ruined her life and hate myself for it. Ruined it by going to a Munch show in London. It's as simple, as absurd, as tragic as that.

Spinning away from the French windows I distract myself with activity, plumping up cushions, snatching one up from the floor by Joe's armchair, sorting the coffee table, tidying the papers and magazines in the rack. Moving on to the other half of the room, allowing myself the limp that I do my best to suppress when Joe and Mim are about, my eye is caught by my guitar, leaning casually against the wall as if waiting for me. I go to it. Run my nails across the strings. Not very melodic, but pleasing. I pick it up by the neck, carry it back to the French windows, sit down on the floor facing out, and set about proving yet again that I have very little idea how to play the fucking thing.

Discussion Questions for readers of
THIS RUINED PLACE

1. What did you expect when you started this book? Was the story how you imagined it would be or did it surprise you?

2. Which character do you think changes the most over the course of the book?

3. Who do you think is the main character of the story?

4. Why do you think Juby insisted on calling Midge by her given name, Evy?

5. Who was your favorite character and what about them made them your favorite?

6. Rouklye is based on a real English village called Tyneham. Had you heard of it before? What did you think of its fate?

7. Edwin tells Midge that Juby's view of the village isn't the only one. Whose version did you relate to more, Edwin's or Juby's?

8. There's a hint of the supernatural in this novel. How did this layer of the story add to the overall tone?

9. Rouklye acts as its own character in a way. What did you learn about Rouklye that was the most interesting or impactful for you?

10. How do you feel the work of Midge's parents fits in with Midge's growing knowledge of Rouklye?

11. At the end, Midge sees a rook in the woods. Do you think it was real or conjured by her imagination given what's happened, and the place itself?

12. Juby reveals a very heavy secret to Midge. Was that fair? Is there someone else he should have told instead?

13. Midge learns that Inger and Edwin have been keeping a secret of their own for many years. When she asks why they never told anyone, Inger says that they 'never quite found the moment.' They all agree to continue keeping the secret. What do you think of that decision? And do you think the revelation changes anything for Midge?

14. Midge destroys the letters she was going to send to Nessa. Will she tell her friend everything about her summer or will she end up keeping some secrets of her own?

15. Tyneham really is available to the public in the month of August. Would you want to visit it? Is its history important and relevant to us today?

16. Were you satisfied with the eventual explanation of the 'almost there boy'?

17. The note that Midge finds on the church door is a facsimile of the one put there in 1943 by Tyneham's evacuating villagers. They left in good faith, thinking that they would return in due course. From our vantage point in history, we know that no one ever returned and the entire valley is under military control to this day. What does this knowledge bring to your reading of the story?

18. Do you think something like this could or would happen today? Why or why not?

19. Do you think what happened to Tyneham is worse, better, or similar to the types of things happening today?

20. *This Ruined Place* has been described as 'haunting' and 'unforgettable'. Is there anything about it that you think will stay with you for quite some time?

www.ingramcontent.com/pod-product-compliance
Lightning Source LLC
Chambersburg PA
CBHW050511260626
47157CB00004B/1278